"He said...he won't stop. He *will* kill me."

The siren was louder. Closer.

Another tear slid down her cheek. "He said he'd been waiting for me...that the waiting was over."

His body brushed against hers. "He's not going to ever touch you again." Josh intended to make sure of that. "You're safe."

But she shook her head, and Josh didn't think she believed him.

The sheriff's patrol car whipped around the corner. The lights flashed from the top of the car.

Casey's hold tightened on Josh even more.

"You're safe," he said again, but Josh knew that she didn't believe him.

HUNTED

———

New York Times Bestselling Author

CYNTHIA EDEN

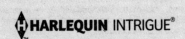

HARLEQUIN INTRIGUE®

I want to thank the wonderful staff at Harlequin—
Denise, Kayla, EVERYONE at Harlequin Intrigue.
It is truly a pleasure working with you.

Recycling programs
for this product may
not exist in your area.

ISBN-13: 978-1-335-72107-5

Hunted

Copyright © 2017 by Cindy Roussos

Printed in U.S.A.

Cynthia Eden is a *New York Times* and *USA TODAY* bestselling author. She writes dark tales of romantic suspense and paranormal romance. Her books have received starred reviews from *Publishers Weekly*, and one was named a 2013 RITA® Award finalist for best romantic suspense. Cynthia lives in the Deep South, loves horror movies and has an addiction to chocolate. More information about Cynthia may be found at www.cynthiaeden.com.

Books by Cynthia Eden

Harlequin Intrigue

Killer Instinct

Abduction
Hunted

The Battling McGuire Boys

Confessions
Secrets
Suspicions
Reckonings
Deceptions
Allegiances

Shadow Agents: Guts and Glory

Undercover Captor
The Girl Next Door
Evidence of Passion
Way of the Shadows

MIRA Books

Killer Instinct

The Gathering Dusk (prequel to *Abduction*)
After the Dark

Visit the Author Profile page at Harlequin.com for more titles.

CAST OF CHARACTERS

Josh Duvane—A former navy SEAL, Josh is part of the FBI's elite Underwater Search and Evidence Response Team (USERT). He travels all over the US as he investigates underwater crime scenes. His latest case takes him to a small coastal town in Florida...and he meets the reporter who will change his world.

Cassandra "Casey" Quinn—Casey is a top-notch television journalist. She's used to reporting the news, not *being* the news. But when Casey escapes an attack from a brutal killer, her life is thrown into chaos. For help, she turns to the only man she can trust—Josh Duvane. But is he hiding dark secrets, too?

Tom Warren—Tom is the producer of Casey's show, and he knows that her attack will mean high ratings with viewers. He's willing to do anything in order to land a major story, even use Casey as bait in a deadly game.

Katrina Welch—Casey's assistant Katrina is working her own agenda. She's tired of playing backup for Casey, and even if she walks into danger, Katrina is ready for her chance in the spotlight.

Tucker Frost—FBI agent Tucker Frost has a dark and twisted past. But does that past make him the perfect person to hunt predators? Or could he be just as dangerous as the criminals that he tracks?

Chapter One

Josh Duvane broke from the surface of the water, pulling the regulator out of his mouth and then shoving back his mask. "We found her," he called to the team up on the boat.

He heard someone swear. Probably the local sheriff. Josh knew the guy had been hoping to find the victim alive. No such luck. Josh swam to the boat. The ocean water lapped against him, dark and rough because a storm was coming. If they were lucky, they'd be able to get the victim up before the storm hit.

A big *if.*

He grabbed for the ladder on the back of the boat and pulled himself up.

"Are you sure it's Tonya?" Sheriff Hayden Black asked as he reached out a hand to Josh.

Tonya. Tonya Myers. The twenty-two-year-old college coed who'd vanished a week ago. And, yes, unfortunately, he was sure. "It's her."

He glanced back at the water. The waves rocked

against the boat. As one of the FBI's elite USERT members—Underwater Search and Evidence Response Team—his job routinely took him to the deepest depths. He searched for clues, he searched for evidence and, on damn unfortunate days—days like today—he searched for the dead.

"That makes three bodies," Hayden gritted out. The waning light glinted off his blond hair. "Three bodies in the last three weeks."

And that was why Josh was there. The FBI knew they had a serial hunting in the quiet coastal town, and Josh had been sent to provide backup to the local Bureau team—and to the sheriff.

Josh and Hayden had crossed paths in the past. Once upon a time, they'd trained together as SEALs. They'd worked together on a few missions years ago, then had gone their separate ways. Josh had joined the FBI and Hayden—hell, Josh never would have figured the guy for a small-town sheriff.

I would have figured wrong.

"This town has already had enough heartache," Hayden muttered. "The people need peace, not more fear."

More divers went into the water. Josh had done his job and located the body. His team would work to bring the victim to the surface.

"We just put one killer behind bars." Hayden raked a hand over his face. The sheriff's star on his uniform gleamed. "Theodore Anderson's trial is barely over. Now some other jerk is terrorizing *my* Hope."

Not just terrorizing the town of Hope, but killing mercilessly. The victims taken were all women in their twenties, attractive, fit. And they weren't locals. Hope was a beach town along the Florida Gulf Coast—popular in the early summer for its pristine white beaches. The victims had been tourists.

The killer had a twisted MO. He took the women, then he immediately called the sheriff's station, taunting the authorities. Telling them to hurry and find the victim before it was too late.

But so far, they'd always been too late. Each victim had been stabbed to death. The first two victims had each been stabbed five times, and then their throats had been slit. Josh was betting that when the ME had a chance to check the body of Tonya Myers, he'd find the same wounds on her.

After he'd dumped his victims in the water, the perp made a second call to the authorities. A brief call that just gave longitude and latitude coordinates. The dump site location for the body.

In Josh's experience, most killers didn't offer up their victims that way. For someone to do that—to deliberately call the authorities and just spill the location of the dead—it meant one thing.

The perp wants attention. He wants the world to know what he's doing.

And the guy was getting that attention. News crews were camped out in Hope, desperately trying to get a scoop on the new case that was transfixing the nation. Murder was always big business.

"He'll be going after a new victim soon," Josh said quietly. His wet suit stretched as he strode to the bow of the boat. "You need your deputies to be on high alert. You need to warn the people in this area to stay extra vigilant. Because if we aren't careful…" His words trailed away. The killer was very careful. He didn't leave evidence behind, none of his taunting calls to the sheriff had been traced back to him…he was always one step ahead of the authorities. "If we aren't careful, soon I'll be searching for another body."

THEY'D FOUND THE VICTIM. Cassandra "Casey" Quinn tensed when she saw the black body bag being unloaded from the boat. "Another one," she whispered as sadness tightened her heart. Another woman who'd been struck down in the small, coastal town.

"Should I start filming?" her camerawoman asked.

She should say yes. The other camera crews were already rolling, capturing the moment when that body bag was transferred out of the boat and onto the stretcher. The ME was there. He'd be taking the body back to his lab.

"Casey?"

How long had the woman been in the water? One day? Two? Tonya Myers had finished up her bachelor's degree at Florida State University just two weeks before. She'd gone to Hope to relax. To have a little fun in the sun.

Not to die.

"We're missing the shot, Casey," Katrina Welch snapped.

Right. The shot. The story. That was why she was down there, after all. Why she'd left New York and flown down to face the already blistering Florida heat. "Keep the camera on me and the sheriff," she directed. *Not the body bag. I just… I can't.* "Maybe I can get him to share an exclusive with me." Doubtful. So far, Hayden Black had been like a vault.

Good thing she was pretty good at safecracking.

There were about half a dozen reporters gathered on the dock. Most of them were filming the body bag. Some were rushing toward the ME, and yes, two others had tried to go after the sheriff. He waved them back. She heard the growl of "No comment" that came from Hayden. Typical. She'd discovered that even though he was a native Florida boy, Hayden wasn't exactly big on the southern charm.

Her gaze darted over him. Tall, blond, strong… the sheriff walked with a furious intensity, his body practically vibrating with tension. He didn't like what was happening in his town. Not one damn bit.

But there was another man with him. Also blond, but his hair was a darker shade, shaggier than the sheriff's. This man moved with a predatory power, and his gaze swept the scene, as if looking for threats. *Dangerous. This guy is seriously dangerous.*

"That's the USERT guy in charge, right?" Katrina asked as she pressed closer. "I think I saw him go out on the boat that retrieved the body."

Victim, not body.

"He looks mad." Katrina lifted her camera and aimed it toward the sheriff. "They both do."

"Probably because they don't like finding dead women." She swallowed. "And, yes, he's USERT. His name's Josh Duvane." As soon as the USERT group had arrived, she'd begun digging up information on them. Digging up information was sort of her thing…almost a compulsion. She didn't even date a guy without doing a full background check, and Casey knew that was weird. But with her past, it paid to be careful. "Ex-SEAL, tough as nails, swims like a fish." And he'd been the guy to find all three of the victims.

She swallowed. "Maybe he's the one who'll talk." Maybe. She smoothed back her dark hair, straightened her already straight blouse and lifted her chin. "Let's just see what happens." Briskly, she walked toward the two men, with Katrina at her heels. "Sheriff Black!" Casey called out brightly. "Can you confirm that the body of Tonya Myers has been recovered?"

Hayden turned toward her, and his golden eyes were sharp with barely leashed fury. "No comment, Ms. Quinn. None."

Figured. The guy was far too tight-lipped.

She lowered her microphone. Voice softer, she said, "Don't you think the public has a right to know what's happening here? People are dying, Sheriff. And if you found Tonya's body, then that means another victim will be taken soon."

He stared at her. Then he gave a grim nod. "Film me."

He'd just said—her eyes widened and she gestured to Katrina. *Film the man. Film the man!* Before he changed his mind.

Hayden stared into the camera lens. "There is a predator hunting in our city. I would like to ask every citizen to be extra vigilant. If you see anything suspicious, please do not hesitate to call the sheriff's office. I am working in conjunction with the FBI to track down and apprehend this criminal, and I ask that all individuals—particularly women in their twenties who may be visiting our area—take every precaution—"

"Is that because the Sandy Shore Killer has a special victim type?" Casey cut in. "He only kills women in their twenties? Women who are vacationing in Hope, not locals?"

His eyes glittered. "Turn off the camera."

Well, at least they'd gotten something. Casey waved toward Katrina and made a quick, slashing motion across her throat.

Katrina's sigh was very, very loud.

"The Sandy Shore Killer?" It wasn't Hayden who'd spoken. It was the FBI agent—the USERT supervisor, Josh Duvane. His voice was deep, dark and sexy. Not that Casey found the guy sexy. She was at a crime scene for goodness sake. She had a job to do. She wasn't there to lust after some agent.

Her gaze swept over Josh Duvane, studying him, assessing him. Tall, over six feet, with broad shoulders. His thick blond hair was still a little wet. His skin was tanned—probably because of all the time he spent in the water—and his hard jaw appeared freshly shaven. He had a faint scar on his right cheek, a slash of white that told her the scar was old. His eyes were hazel. Not a warm and cozy hazel, though. They were stone-cold.

Chilling, she would say.

Or maybe that was just the look he was giving her. *Like an ice glare. He's freezing me out.* Because if Casey had to guess, she'd say that FBI Agent Josh Duvane did *not* like her very much. A pity. When sources didn't like her, they had a tendency not to share information. She really needed him to share.

"Who the hell gave the guy the moniker of the Sandy Shore Killer?" Josh wanted to know.

She nodded briskly. "That would be me."

He rolled his eyes and cursed. "Lady, giving the guy attention—"

"Cassandra. Or Casey. Either one works."

His lips—rather sensual lips, nicely sculpted—pressed into a thin line. "Giving the guy attention… giving him a freaking *name*…does nothing but feed into his fantasy. You're building him up when we want to be tearing him down."

She didn't let her expression alter. Casey hadn't

wanted to give the guy a nickname, but her producer had insisted. "You can only call a guy the *unknown perpetrator* for so long, you realize that, right?" She gestured to the beach behind them. "And he *does* place his victims in the water off the sandy shores here. It seemed fitting at the time." The name had certainly stuck.

"Vultures like you just do more damage." Josh turned away from her. "You don't help anyone."

She didn't flinch, but his words shot straight to her heart.

Josh and the sheriff headed toward the parking lot.

"I'm not trying to do damage." Maybe she should have kept her mouth shut but…no, he'd just insulted her. Casey figured that she deserved a chance to defend herself. "I'm trying to help this investigation. I'm trying to *help* the victims. They deserve justice."

Josh put his hand on the sheriff's shoulder. He leaned in close and said something quietly to Hayden. The sheriff nodded and then strode to his patrol car.

Josh turned to glance back at her.

"If looks could kill," Katrina muttered, "I think you'd be dead on the ground right about now."

Casey swallowed. She thought Katrina might be right. If possible, Josh's gaze had grown even colder. "Why don't you go back to the hotel? I'll meet you in a little while."

Katrina nodded and hurried away. She took the camera—and Casey's microphone—with her. Katrina's red hair was cut short, a pixie cut that accentuated her delicate features. But there was nothing delicate about Katrina's personality. The woman was a fireball, and Casey normally loved working with her.

Right then, though, she wanted some space. If she had a chance to speak alone with Josh, she might be able to convince him that she wasn't the bad guy.

Possibly.

Josh crossed his arms over his chest and studied Casey in silence. She wondered what he was thinking. What did he see when—

"Are high heels really the best choice for the beach?"

She glanced down at her heels. No, they were a terrible choice for the beach. Wretched. But when she'd left the hotel earlier, Casey hadn't realized she'd be *going* to the beach. She'd thought that she would see Hayden Black at the sheriff's station. She'd known she'd be on camera, so she'd had to wear what she thought of as her full reporter getup.

She walked toward him and her high heels wobbled a bit on the uneven pavement of the parking lot. The lot was right in front of the dock—and the stretching, white sand beach waited to the right. The scent of the ocean teased her nose.

"I don't want to be your enemy," she said and she gave him what she hoped was a warm smile. She'd practiced that smile a lot when she first started reporting. That smile had taken her from a spot in small-town Illinois to the big-league fame of a prime-time show in New York City. Her smile was warm. Friendly. Approachable. That was her deal—her producer said she was relatable. That she came across as caring.

The truth was…she really did care. Often, far too much. She couldn't turn off the cases that she covered, and late at night, when she was alone, they haunted her. "I'm *not* the bad guy."

"Didn't say you were." His head cocked as she approached him.

"You just thought it." She inclined her head. "And you *did* say I was a vulture."

The other reporters were clearing out. The ME had left. The body had been transferred. The sheriff was gone.

Other than a few stragglers at the lot, she was left with Josh.

"I've seen your work before," Josh murmured. "I know plenty about you, Ms. Quinn."

"Cassandra," she corrected quickly. "Or—"

"Casey, right."

His expression was so hard and unyielding. He was a handsome man, but…tough. A dangerous vibe seemed to pulse just beneath his skin.

"You don't seem to have a lot of respect for reporters," she murmured, though she rather thought her words were a serious understatement.

He looked at her, considering, and then his gaze darted to the water behind her. He rolled back his wide shoulders and sighed. Some of the tension appeared to leave him. His face didn't soften but it seemed less…angry? "You know what? It's my baggage, and I'm sorry."

Wait—he was what?

"I'm being a jackass to you, and I apologize." He sounded as if he meant those words. "It's been a hell of a day, and when I find—"

He broke off, but she knew what he'd been about to say. *When I find a body…*

"I'm not at my best," Josh finished as he raked a hand over his face. "But I shouldn't be a jerk to you, and I apologize."

"Apology accepted," she said quietly.

He gave her a quick, searching glance. "May I tell you a story, Ms. Quinn?"

"Casey—"

He stepped toward her and her breath caught. He was…definitely strong. He wore a white T-shirt and shorts and she knew he'd changed out of his diving gear on the boat. The muscles of his arms and chest stretched the fabric of that T-shirt. He didn't look like the typical, straitlaced FBI agent.

Probably because he wasn't.

"A few months ago, I worked a real big case over in Fairhope, Alabama. We were after the Sorority Slasher…you remember that one?"

Her heart shoved into her throat. "Everyone remembers him."

"Another stupid serial killer name. Folks should have just said they were looking for Dr. Cameron

Latham, the genius psychology professor who decided killing was just too much fun." His lips twisted into a bitter smile. "A reporter from that area was covering the case, trying to get all the headlines and make a name for herself."

The breath she took seemed to chill her lungs. "I—I know what happened to the reporter." *Everyone knows.* Because a story that terrible wasn't easily forgotten.

"No, you *know* what was reported. You *know* that Dr. Latham killed the reporter. He wanted to send a message, and she was the perfect target. That's what people know. But I was there." He edged even closer to her. His body brushed against hers as he lowered his head—and his voice. "I know exactly what he did to her. And everything I'm about to say is off the record."

She should back away. Put some distance between them. But she just looked up into his eyes. *He's trying to intimidate me. I won't let him.*

"I saw the blood-soaked room. I saw the body. I saw the way he'd wrecked her. He enjoyed hurting her, and her last moments—they were just of terror and pain. He left her alive in that room, you see. He let her know that death was coming, and there was nothing she could do to stop it."

Casey licked her lips. Her mouth felt desert dry.

"So, yeah, I'm a little…sensitive to reporters right now. Because I think that reporter—Janice Beautfont—her death was a waste. She pushed herself into the spotlight, and he made her a victim. So when I see the reporters crowding around, wanting to spread the sick stories of *this* killer's crimes…I remember Janice, and I hate what happened to her. I hate that this guy is feeding off the attention he's getting, and I wish you would all just take a step back."

Her skin felt too cold. It was a summer day on the Florida coast. *Cold* was the last thing she should be feeling. "I'm not trying to be in the spotlight."

He raised one brow.

She swallowed the lump in her throat. "You don't know me. I get that. But you're *wrong* here. I want the focus on the victims. I want them to have justice."

"That's why I'm here," he murmured. "And it's always easier to do my job when I don't have a reporter dogging my steps."

So much for having a partnership with him. Desperate, she tried again as she said, "I can help you. I've been talking to the victims' family members and their friends. I know things about the victims. Maybe I can help build a profile—"

"We have agents from our Behavioral Analysis Unit who do that."

He was definitely shutting her down.

"Watch your step, Ms. Quinn," he said again, but she knew he wasn't talking about her high heels and the broken pavement in the parking lot. "Because you never know when a killer is close."

And the guy just turned and walked away from her.

Her right foot tapped on that uneven pavement.

"Casey," she called after him. "My name is Casey. Remember it—because you'll be seeing me again." If he thought she was just going to give up, the guy needed to think again. She wasn't going to be scared away.

Giving up wasn't in her personality.

If Josh Duvane wouldn't help her, well, then she'd just go find someone else who'd be ready to talk. A good reporter never gave up.

And Casey didn't just want to be good at her job. She wanted to be great.

THEY'D FOUND TONYA. He'd watched as the reporters and the authorities slowly loaded into their vehicles and left the scene. They'd found her faster than they'd discovered his last victim.

But then, he hadn't taken Tonya as far out this time. He'd left her closer to the shore, a deliberate choice. He'd needed to dump her body quickly and then get ready for the next kill.

He already had a new victim in mind.

He could see his prey right then.

She stood in the middle of the parking lot, tapping one high heel. Her dark brown hair fell to her shoulders, a sleek style that even the humidity of Florida couldn't seem to muss. She had on a crisp white shirt and a formfitting black pencil skirt.

She was pretty…almost perfectly so with her fine-drawn features. He'd studied her often enough; he knew every detail of her face. Her wide-set, dark eyes, her bow-shaped mouth, her softly curved chin. He'd watched her on the news, marveling at the way she seemed to stare *right at him*.

As if she could see him.

I see you. He'd seen her all along. He'd seen everything she'd done. All the secrets she'd tried to keep. All the sins that she thought no one knew about...he'd seen everything.

She thought she was safe. She thought no one knew what she'd done.

But he knew.

He'd always known.

And before he was done with her, she'd be begging to tell the world her story.

They always begged.

And then they died.

Chapter Two

Casey sidled around the back of the sheriff's station. Sure, this wasn't exactly her best moment, sneaking up to the back of the building because she knew that the young deputy, Finn Patrick, was scheduled to get off work at eight o'clock that night. But Finn had been kind enough to share a little inside information with her before and she was hoping that he might feel similarly inclined again…

The back door squeaked open. It was a heavy metal door, and it led from the rear of the station to the small staff parking lot in the back.

Casey made sure her friendly smile was in place as that door opened. She stood in the shadows, waiting to see Finn's dark hair appear but—

Blond hair.

Her smile froze. She expected Sheriff Hayden Black to exit the building.

But the man who came out *wasn't* Hayden. The blond hair was a little too dark.

Josh Duvane shut the door behind him. He tensed

and his gaze swept toward the right—toward the shadows. Toward her.

He'd changed his clothes again, and now the guy looked more like an FBI agent. Khaki pants, button-down shirt and a holster. A holster that he was currently reaching for as he kept his narrow-eyed gaze in her direction.

"Wait!" Casey called out. She hurried forward with a clatter of her—yes, still wearing them—heels. "It's just me."

If anything, his expression became even darker. "Should have known you'd be skulking around."

"Skulking?" Casey repeated, not liking that particular word choice.

"Yeah, skulking. Hanging around, hoping for a weak link to appear so you can get another scoop." He put his hands on his lean hips. "I know Finn tipped you off last time." Josh gave a sad shake of his head. "You like preying on twenty-year-old deputies? The guy is green and you know it. You got him to spill confidential information to you that could jeopardize the case."

Furious, she kept marching toward him. "I didn't jeopardize anything! Finn just told me the number of stab wounds that the victims suffered—"

"And you immediately reported it, opening the door for copycats galore to come out and play."

Her breath heaved out. "You don't like me." Were they really back to that already?

"I don't know you, as you pointed out earlier."

His gaze swept the dark lot. "And, lady, why would you want to be out here by yourself? You know you match the killer's victim profile, right?"

"I—" Yes, okay, maybe she did know that. But she was at the *sheriff's station.* Shouldn't that be the safest spot in town?

He grabbed her wrist, surprising her. It wasn't the quick movement itself that surprised her. Rather, she was surprised by how gentle his touch was. His hand wrapped around her wrist, and she felt the faint caress of his fingertips against her pulse point.

A little shiver slid over her.

"Sheriff Black gave advice for folks to be vigilant. He gave that advice to *you.* And what do you do? You immediately run out and find the first dimly lit, empty parking lot that you can?"

"I know how to take care of myself."

"I'm sure the other victims thought that, too." His gaze slid around the lot. "Where the hell is your car?"

"My hotel is four blocks away. I just walked—"

"Because you have a death wish?"

She silently counted to ten, then said, "You are getting on my bad side."

He smiled at her, a quick flash that showed the dimple—no, not really dimple, more like a rough slant—in his right cheek. "When you get angry, your voice goes absolutely arctic."

Then she must be completely freezing him right then.

"Finn isn't coming out here. He's pulling a second

shift and, even if he weren't, the sheriff just gave him orders not to speak to *any* reporter, including pretty brunettes who smell like candy."

Her eyes widened. "Smell like—candy?"

"Didn't realize that, huh? You do."

Her cheeks were burning.

He turned away, but kept his grip on her wrist and he pulled her toward the far side of the lot. A motorcycle waited there, a big black beast of a bike.

"I'll give you a lift to your hotel. See, I can be a *nice* guy."

He climbed onto the motorcycle and tried to tug her on after him. Casey locked her knees and refused to budge.

He sighed. He seemed to do that a lot around her. "Problem?"

"I don't like motorcycles." Yes, she sounded prim and disapproving. So what? She wasn't sure she liked him, either. She certainly didn't like his ride. "They go too fast. They flip too easily. They offer zero protection to the rider—"

"Not a risk taker, huh? Guess I pegged that part wrong about you." His gaze dropped down her body and stopped on her three-inch shoes. "It's the heels. When a woman wears sexy heels like that, it makes a guy think she may have an…adventurous side."

"Are you hitting on me? Or insulting me again?" She wanted to be clear. "Because earlier, you said I was a vulture. Now you're saying—"

He let go of her wrist, but only so that he could

hand her a helmet. "This will protect your head and that pretty face of yours."

"You are hitting on me." She took the helmet. She did *not* get on the motorcycle. "Your routine needs work. A lot of it."

"I did a little research on you since our last meeting…"

Her hold tightened on the helmet. *Don't have dug too deep. Don't have found—*

"You've won a lot of awards, haven't you? Seems you're the investigative journalist to watch. And you make a habit of going after the darkest killers, don't you?"

Her heart was drumming too fast and hard in her chest. "I go where I'm needed. You might not like the work I do, but someone has to give the victims a voice."

"And that's what you do."

It's what she tried to do.

He revved the engine. The bike sounded like a giant, growling beast. "You said your hotel was four blocks away. Hardly far enough of a distance for me to go too fast on that short drive. And if you're with me…" He gave her that slow smile again, the one that made him look a little less dangerous. Only a little. "I'll be extra careful. I promise."

She looked around the parking lot. It *was* getting darker. A lot darker. And, yes, she did fit the victim profile; she knew it. She was the right age, a stranger, no close ties in Hope… "Don't go over the speed limit."

He laughed. It was a strangely warm sound that caught her off guard. "I'm FBI. Trust me—I've got this."

She climbed onto the motorcycle. Her skirt hiked up—up much higher than she'd anticipated—and she knew she was flashing thigh. Her heels settled along the bike, finding safe purchase. She put on the helmet and then her hands kind of fluttered in the air. Should she put them behind her? There was a bar back there. She should probably just grab on to it and hold tight.

"Hold on to me."

She'd been afraid he'd say that. Casey slowly wrapped her arms around him.

"Tighter."

Why? "I thought you said you weren't going fast."

"You still need to hold tight, Casey." It was the first time he'd said her name. It came out rumbly and sexy and she needed to *stop* thinking the guy was sexy.

He was an FBI agent working a case.

She was a reporter.

She might try to work *him* to get information, but they were not going to have any sort of real, personal relationship. She didn't *do* personal relationships. She kept her distance from people for many, many reasons.

Fumbling a bit, her hands slid around his waist, but she didn't hold *that* tight.

"Tell me the name of your hotel."

There were several just up the road—a line of them that looked out over the beach. "West Winds."

She would *not* hold him tighter.

The motorcycle shot forward and her arms tightened around him, holding him in a death grip and smashing her body against his. He zipped through the town, not actually going too fast but...it was strange being on the motorcycle with him. The wind whipped at her, and the motorcycle vibrated beneath her. He was strong and solid in front of her, and Casey found herself thinking that...maybe, if it were a different time, if this were a different place...she and the FBI agent might not have found themselves being adversaries.

They might have been something a whole lot more fun.

Too soon, he was braking in front of her hotel. Other reporters were staying at the hotel, at least five she knew from previous jobs. And both her producer and her camerawoman were there—plenty of people that she knew. It was a safe place.

Josh killed the engine and put down the kickstand. She realized she was still holding him, and Casey let go quickly, nearly jumping from the motorcycle. Josh didn't move, but she could feel his gaze sweeping over her. A bit nervously, Casey pushed the helmet back at him. "Th-thank you." She hated that stutter.

She *never* stuttered. Or at least, she worked hard to make sure she didn't. When she'd been younger, that stutter had always come out when she'd been afraid. Back then, she'd had plenty to fear. The nightmares had plagued her every night for a solid year during college.

He put the helmet on the back of the bike. He studied her a moment and the waves crashed in the distance.

Should she just walk away? Probably.

"You don't think it's odd?"

"What?" She wasn't sure she followed him.

"All of you reporters…" He gestured to the hotel behind her and she knew he'd realized other press personnel were staying in that same location. "You all came rushing down here weeks ago to cover the Theodore Anderson case."

Theodore Anderson. She crossed her arms over her chest. Yes, he'd been the reason she was first sent to Hope. He'd been arrested and linked to the abduction and disappearance of several young girls in the area. Many of the crimes had occurred *years* ago, but only recently had he been linked to the kills.

The saddest part of the case? At least to Casey? The man had killed his own daughter. Christy Anderson had been murdered by her father when she was just thirteen years old.

Theodore had made headlines when he was arrested, and, yes, the reporters had all flocked down to cover the case when he went to trial. He'd been found guilty on all counts, and Theodore Anderson would never see the light of day again. Originally, the press had focused on Theodore, but it hadn't been long before someone else started stealing the Front Page...

The Sandy Shore Killer.

"What are the odds," Josh continued in that deep voice of his, "that in this sleepy little town, there would be not just one sadistic killer...but two?"

She licked her lips. "Considering how rare serial killers are...I'd say those odds should be astronomically low. But then...you're FBI. You should know better than I do."

"They *are* astronomically low. Coincidences like this one don't happen." Flat.

"But...it is happening."

"Something set this guy off. Something brought him here..." His head turned and he gazed at the hotel behind her. "Can't help but wonder...if it was you."

She backed up a step. *He knows. He dug into my past. He dug too deep. He found out what I did—*

"You and all the reporters," he continued as his hazel gaze slid back to her. "He didn't like the fame that Theodore Anderson was getting, so he decided to steal the spotlight. And you and your buddies— with your twenty-four-seven news coverage—you just fed his beast. You made him more determined to get the attention he wanted."

Casey shook her head. "You think this guy came

here because of the reporters? Is *that* the theory the FBI is running with?"

His hand lifted and his fingers curved under her cheek. "We're off the record. Way, way off…"

His fingers were faintly callused, a little rough against her skin.

"As I said, it's highly unlikely we'd have *two* serial killers in the same town. That just doesn't happen. Serial killers are rare to begin with and this… it isn't by chance. Your 'Sandy Shore Killer' was drawn here for a reason."

"Have the victims been connected in any way?" She had to press for more details.

"You know about the victims already. Attractive women in their twenties, all single, all visiting the area—no close personal ties here. And that's all I will say about them now."

His hand dropped away from her cheek and curved back around his handlebar. He revved the engine again.

Right. He was leaving. "Thanks for the ride."

His gaze raked over her. She wondered… Did he feel that odd, thick tension between them? The heated attraction that seemed to fill the air?

His hazel stare burned.

He did.

"Good night, Casey."

He felt the attraction, but Josh just wasn't going to do anything about it. Those rule-following FBI guys. They weren't her type. Or at least, they shouldn't be.

"I'll wait until you're inside before I leave." He paused a beat. "A gentleman never leaves before a lady is safely inside."

"Is that what you are? A gentleman?"

He seemed to consider that. "Perhaps I could be whatever you want me to be."

Casey turned away and hurried up the steps that led to the hotel. When she was in the lobby, she glanced back at him. He was still sitting on the motorcycle, still staring at her. Still looking far too sexy.

She lifted her hand and waved.

He frowned, gave her a small wave back, then drove away.

A few people who she recognized filled the lobby, and she inclined her head toward them as she headed for the elevator. The doors dinged open and when she slipped inside, Casey immediately ditched her heels. *So much better.* When she reached her floor, she carried her shoes in one hand, letting them dangle and bump against her leg. She was on the top floor, one that gave her a great view of the beach. She used her key card and slipped inside. The room was dark and ice-cold because she'd left the air-conditioning unit on earlier that day.

Casey turned on the light by the door. The maid had been in to clean—the room was spotless. Her pillows were all fluffed. New towels were waiting and the room had a fresh, lemony scent. She dropped her shoes and headed for the balcony door. She flipped the lock on it and slipped outside. The crash of the waves hit her first. The sound, then the scent. Stars glittered in the distance and she could see a handful of people walking on the beach.

She stood there a moment, lost in the sight. It didn't seem right for something so beautiful to be linked to so much death. But if she'd learned anything in life…it was that beauty often hid darkness. A smile hid terror. Pain always waited. So did evil.

She turned from the view and reached for the balcony door. But…

Hadn't she turned on the light in her room? Because the interior was pitch-black. She could see the darkness through the glass.

I turned it on when I walked inside. I always do that.

At least, she thought she had. But maybe there was a short or some kind of electrical problem. She'd have to call the front desk if there was trouble.

She opened the door and slipped inside. A little light spilled in from behind her, providing enough illumination for her to make her way to the small table near the bed. There was a lamp waiting there. She'd turn it on and then—

Hard hands wrapped around her from behind just as a bitter, thick odor hit her. "Got you."

She opened her mouth to scream, but her attacker drove her forward, slamming her head into the wall just above the lamp. The impact was hard and she staggered. Casey didn't get to scream. She didn't even get to fight.

He rammed her head into the wall a second time.
Just like before...
No!
Her body was going limp. She was passing out.
His rough laughter was the last sound she heard.

Chapter Three

He drove for miles, just riding the motorcycle and
letting the wind brush across his face. In his head, he
kept reliving the day's dive. Sinking deep beneath the
water, searching even as he hoped that he wouldn't
find the body. He'd hoped that the victim was still
alive. That she still had a chance.

Then he'd seen her hair. That was the way it often
was on those dives. If he was searching for a woman,
her hair would float up from her head. It would drift
in the water around her, as if it were trying to reach
out for the surface.

He'd seen Tonya's hair, then he'd seen her face.
Not the pretty face from her picture—chalk white,
bloated.

Dead.

He turned off his engine and sat near the edge
of the beach, almost surprised to find himself so
close to Casey's hotel. He hadn't meant to come back
there, had he?

Casey Quinn.

He'd seen her news stories before, most folks had. She didn't work for some local channel—Casey was the big time. Prime-time TV on a major network. When he'd done some digging on her, he'd realized her pieces were always dark, focusing on the worst criminals out there. Not scare pieces, though, but reports that showed the broken lives that had been left in a monster's wake.

He knew she'd come down to Hope to cover Theodore Anderson's case—the sick freak had enjoyed kidnapping girls. Kidnapping them and killing them. He'd even killed his own daughter. Casey and the other reporters had been trying to interview both Theodore Anderson and the guy's son, Kurt. But Kurt hadn't talked to *any* reporters. Not yet. Josh was a bit surprised that Casey's charm hadn't worked on the guy. Her smile—yeah, he could see where she'd be able to get men to talk to her. That slow smile was pure sex appeal, and it did something to her eyes— made those dark chocolate eyes gleam. No wonder young Finn had overshared, but the deputy knew better now. Josh and Hayden had made *certain* the kid knew better.

He turned away from the beach and glanced up at her hotel. He'd touched her cheek and her skin had been like silk beneath his hand. She'd stood there, in those incredibly sexy heels, her skin a warm gold next to the white of her shirt, and that dark hair of hers had skimmed over her shoulders. She was small, built along delicate lines, but sure curved in

every perfect place. When she'd been behind him
on the bike—

*Stop lusting, turn on the motorcycle and get out
of here.*

He wasn't going to cross any lines with the reporter. A sexy face and body weren't going to make
him forget his job. He wasn't young Finn.

He rolled back his shoulders.

Get out of here.

But he couldn't help glancing at the hotel just one
more time.

SHE HURT.

Casey groaned as she cracked open one eyelid.
Her whole body ached and she was lying on something rough and hard. The hotel bed was normally
soft, like falling into a cloud after a long day of work,
but this—

I'm not at the hotel.

Both of her eyes flew open. She stared around,
horrified. She wasn't in her hotel. She was... Where
in the hell *was* she? She tried to move her body and
realized that her hands and feet were tied. Her hands
were behind her back and she could feel what felt like
rough hemp rope cutting into her wrists. She twisted
and her body slid over...over plastic?

Yes, she was on a big sheet of plastic. The smell of
fresh wood filled the air, and her frantic glance took
in the room around her. She was in a home...of some
sort. One that appeared to be under construction. No

Sheetrock was up on the walls yet. She could see the wooden framework all around her.

And I'm on plastic. Oh, God. Because she *knew* why an abductor would put his prey on plastic. *So there won't be a mess left behind when he's done with me.*

She wiggled and twisted and finally managed to sit up. When she did, she realized that light was pouring in through one of the windows to the right. Light, and she could also hear the thunder of waves. *I'm on the beach. In a house under construction. A house or some kind of condo complex or...*

No, it's a beach house. Because she remembered seeing about four houses that had been under construction on the west end of the beach. They'd been big, massive structures up on wooden stilts that screamed high-end real estate. But, if the place was under construction, where were the construction workers? Where was the crew? Where was someone who could— "Help!" Casey called out. Her voice was oddly weak, so she tried again, screaming, *"Help!"* with all of her strength.

She fought to remember what had happened to her. She'd been in her hotel room and then...*someone* had been there. He'd grabbed her. Rammed her head into the wall—jabbed her? Injected her with something? And she'd fallen. Everything had gone dark. But she thought that she remembered him...laughing.

The waves kept thundering. Her gaze narrowed on the window. There was only a little light coming in. Maybe dawn hadn't fully arrived yet. Since it wasn't dawn, that meant the work crew wouldn't be coming for a while and—

It's Sunday. Her eyes squeezed closed. No, the work crew wouldn't be arriving anytime soon.

She jerked and twisted her way across the room. The plastic slid beneath her, bunching up, and she tried not to think about it—or about the man who'd taken her. The man who could appear any moment. The man who—

"I heard you screaming, Casey Quinn."

She froze. Casey didn't want to look over her shoulder. *He* was back there. If she looked at him, if she saw his face—

"Guess your screams mean…it's time to get started."

And she had to look back. Her head jerked toward him. He stood in the framed doorway. Dressed head to toe in black—complete with a black ski mask that covered his face. She couldn't even see his eyes because there was some kind of weird mesh over them. "Stay away from me," she ordered, hating that her voice shook.

He laughed—the laugh that she remembered—and he pulled out a knife.

The plastic beneath me…it's to catch all of the blood.

"Can't stay away," he told her. "I have work to do."

"Y-you're going to stab me…five times?" Because that was what he did. With all of his victims, he stabbed them. And then he slit their throats and dumped the bodies in the ocean.

I fit his profile. Josh even said... No, no, this couldn't happen!

He came toward her, moving slowly. He bent and brought the knife toward her. She heaved and strained against the ropes, but they wouldn't give. He put the knife to her cheek. Pressed just enough that a drop of blood slid down her face. "Don't rush me," he murmured. "I've been waiting for this moment a long time."

What?

"You and I are going to talk. You're going to tell me all of your secrets."

No, she wasn't.

"Or I will cut you open."

He lifted the blade away from her face—the moment she'd been waiting for. He was crouched close to her—his mistake. He thought that just because she was tied up, she was helpless.

He was wrong.

She lifted her feet—*wish I still had on my heels, those spikes would have come in handy*—and she slammed them right into his crotch, as hard as she could. He gave a grunt and staggered back. The knife fell from his fingers. She grabbed it, rolling and slamming her body harder into the plastic. The blade cut her fingers, but she didn't care. She started sawing at the ropes that bound her wrists together and—

He drove his fist into her cheek, so hard that she

saw stars. The knife fell from her fingers as her head slammed back and hit the plastic—and the hard wood beneath it.

He swore and grabbed her by the hair, yanking her toward him. As he hauled her up, her hands fumbled across the floor and something sliced into her pinky finger…something sharp and narrow.

A nail. A nail was sticking up through the wood.

"Don't go passing out on me. We have to make a phone call. That's step one for us. Got to let folks know who has the power here."

She kept her hands near that nail and started to slide the rope against it. Was it making a grinding noise as she sawed? Could he hear her? The knife's blade had almost cut all the way through the rope, and if the nail could just finish the job, then she'd have a chance.

He left her there, sagging on the floor, her hands behind her and working slowly with that nail as he yanked a phone out of his back pocket. Her gaze darted to his hands. He was wearing gloves, but she could see a little bit of tanned skin where the gloves ended near his wrists. The guy was Caucasian, a little over six feet, probably close to one hundred and eighty pounds, and he—

"I've got someone new," he rasped into the phone. "Pretty soon, Sheriff Black, it will be time for you to find her."

He'd called the sheriff. Did he always do that? Always call while the victim was still alive? The authorities hadn't revealed that detail to the press, and if this was part of the guy's MO, then no wonder Hayden Black had looked increasingly worn. He'd been fighting to find the victims alive, but he kept turning up dead bodies.

His finger slid over the phone—she realized he must be wearing those smart gloves that allowed him to still work a phone screen—and she heard Hayden's voice fill the room.

"Give me proof of life," Hayden barked.

Her abductor laughed. She tensed and almost stopped cutting on that nail. *Almost.* She knew his laughter wasn't a good sign. Hayden wanted proof of life, so that probably meant the jerk in the ski mask was about to make her scream. He was going to hurt her again—

"It's Casey Quinn!" she screamed. *"He's got me in one of the houses under construction on the west end—help—"*

Her abductor threw the phone down and slapped his hand over her mouth. What? Had he believed she didn't realize where she was? When she'd arrived in Hope, she'd made a point of checking out the entire town. A good reporter learned her territory.

She glared up at him.

"Think you're clever?"

She thought she had a chance. Hayden would come racing to the scene. And maybe…maybe he'd get there fast enough to save her.

"Your mistake. You're just dead."

No, she wasn't. Not yet. Did he think she was too afraid to fight back?

She felt the ropes give way around her wrists. Her hands were free. Now she needed to get rid of the ropes around her ankles. She stared up at him, just seeing the mesh over his eyes. Her heartbeat thundered in her chest.

His hand slowly fell from her mouth.

"You should run," she whispered. "The sheriff will be here soon."

"I'm not going anywhere…" He turned away from her. Bent and picked up his phone. She could see the smashed screen. "Not yet." His back was to her.

The knife was on the floor. He hadn't picked it up after he'd punched her. Her hand flew out and grabbed it and she immediately tucked it behind her body, resuming her position as he turned back toward her so it would appear as if her hands were still bound behind her.

"I've waited too long to get you, Casey." His voice was rougher and his tone was almost intimate. "It won't end like this."

It's not going to end at all. She hadn't fought her way back from the darkness before to die this way.

He rolled back his shoulders and he moved a few feet away, his head tilted toward the floor. He lifted up a piece of plastic. *What are you looking for? The knife? Did you just realize it's gone?*

His head swiveled back toward her.

She lifted her chin.

He smiled. "Give it to me." He took a step toward her.

Since he asked…

He grabbed for her arm.

She stabbed him.

THE SOB HAD taken Casey.

Fear was a cold knot in Josh's stomach. Hayden had called him and told him the news, and he'd driven fast as hell to get to the line of houses under construction on the west end of the beach. The motorcycle howled as he raced down the road. He was ahead of the sheriff and his deputies—he'd been closer to the scene. And he was breaking every traffic law out there as he cut across roads and ran through lights to get to Casey.

I shouldn't have left her. He could still see her, standing in front of the hotel, wearing those high heels as her dark hair tossed around her cheeks. He'd even told her that he'd wanted her to be safe because that perp was still out there. The guy was hunting women like her.

He'd been hunting her.

Josh spun around a tight corner and saw the row of partially built houses up ahead. Which house was she in? He barely braked his bike—just jumped off the motorcycle and ran for the first house. "Casey!" Josh roared her name. He yanked his gun from the holster. "Casey, where are you?" *Be alive. Be alive, Casey. Answer me!*

Because in his mind, he still saw Tonya Myers. She was in the water and her dark hair drifted up around her face. *That can't happen to Casey.*

He rushed through the first house, shoving plastic out of his way. Construction debris was everywhere, but the rooms were empty. No sign of Casey.

Josh ran back outside. The light from dawn swept out over the water. *"Casey!"*

How long had it been since the perp had called Hayden? Ten minutes? Fifteen? Twenty?

It only took a moment to die. One moment.

He rushed toward the second house.

"H-help..."

He froze. That call—it had come from the house before him. A temporary door was in place, one without a doorknob, and he just kicked that damn thing in. "Casey!" His bellow seemed to echo around him.

And then he saw her.

She was holding on to the makeshift banister that had been put in place on the stairs. She was trying to come down to him. A red imprint marked the left side of her beautiful face. There was blood on her cheek. She was too pale and she was shaking and—

He bounded toward her.

Her eyes widened when she saw him. She lifted her hand toward him, and he saw that she was gripping a blood-covered knife.

"J-Josh?"

"You're safe." He wanted to scoop her into his

arms. Wanted to hold her tight and make sure she was okay. "Where is he?"

She blinked. She looked lost. Scared. And...

Hurt. He hurt her.

Josh wanted to kill the guy.

"I—I don't know." She looked around, her hand shaking but not letting go of that knife. "He... I stabbed him and he ran out of the room. He...left me."

Grim pride swelled inside of him.

"Get me out of here," she whispered. A tear leaked down her cheek. "It's too much...like before. Get me out."

He didn't know what she was talking about, but he had to touch her. Josh curled his left arm around her as he pulled her against his body. She didn't let go of the knife. He kept a solid grip on his gun. If the perp had run from the room on the upper floor, he could still be hiding in that house. Josh wanted to search every inch of the place, but getting Casey to safety was his priority.

She felt so delicate against him. And each time her body trembled, the rage he felt grew.

I will find you, you bastard. I will make you pay.

He led her past the broken front door and outside. He didn't stop walking, not until they were near his motorcycle. Then he slid his hand under her chin. "Where are you hurt?" His voice was a rough growl. Her cheek was already darkening, the pink giving way to a bruise.

"I'm...okay." Her eyes said the words were a lie. Her head turned, and she looked around the scene. Her voice became a whisper as she said, "Where did he go?"

Josh intended to find out.

Before he could speak, he heard the approaching wail of a siren. The local sheriff and his deputies—about time. They'd search every inch of those houses. They'd find that perp.

He started to step away from Casey but her hand grabbed his wrist. Her fingers curled around him, holding tight. "He's going to kill me."

The hell he will.

"He said...he won't stop. He *will* kill me."

The siren was louder. Closer.

Another tear slid down her cheek. "He said he'd been waiting for me...that the waiting was over."

His body brushed against hers. "He's not going to ever touch you again." Josh intended to make sure of that. "You're safe."

But she shook her head, and Josh knew that she didn't believe him.

The sheriff's patrol car whipped around the corner. The lights flashed from the top of the car.

Casey's hold tightened on Josh even more.

"You're safe," he said again, but Josh didn't think she believed him.

Chapter Four

She was the story.

Casey hunched her shoulders as she sat in the back of the ambulance. The EMT had checked her out thoroughly, over her protests. The guy wanted her to go to the hospital, and she figured he'd be forcing her there soon enough. After all, she knew the routine. She'd have to be examined, evidence would have to be taken from her. They'd clean beneath her nails, they'd take her clothes, they'd—

"Tell me what happened."

Her gaze lifted and she saw Hayden standing at the back of the ambulance. The doors were open and the fury on his face was undeniable. The sheriff was definitely not so controlled any longer.

And neither was Josh. Josh stood beside Hayden, and the FBI agent's face appeared carved from stone. His eyes blazed as he stared at her.

The FBI and the local authorities had been searching the scene, but they hadn't found the man who'd taken her. He'd just...vanished.

She saw a coast guard ship out on the water, darting around. Did they think the perp had escaped by sea? She didn't remember hearing the roar of a boat. She'd just heard the growl of a motorcycle—Josh, rushing to the scene. *I will never fear motorcycles again.*

"Casey," Josh said her name softly. "Look at me."

Her gaze slid back to him. She was sitting on the stretcher in the ambulance. The space was too small. There were too many little machines and the place smelled of antiseptic.

"Tell us what happened."

She already had, hadn't she? At least once? Maybe twice. But if they wanted to hear the story again... Casey pushed back her hair with a weary hand.

Josh swore and he bounded into the ambulance with her.

"Your wrists..."

Oh, right. Those were bandaged, too.

His hands caught hers, his touch incredibly gentle. His tenderness kept surprising her. He seemed so rough. Not a guy who could use such care, but when he touched her, he always seemed to handle her as if she were delicate glass.

She wasn't, though. Far from it. Her gaze darted to her bandaged wrists. "The rope was tight and when I cut myself free, I sliced the skin a bit." She hadn't even felt the pain at the time. Her gaze shifted back to his face. Her shoulders rolled back in a shrug, as if to say... *Doesn't matter.*

Josh glanced at the watchful EMT. "Give us a minute."

The EMT hurried out, but stopped to say, "I'm ready to take her to the hospital and—"

"And I'm not done with my witness," Hayden cut in. "You heard the agent. We need a minute."

The EMT nodded, ducking his head as he backed away.

Josh's fingers slid carefully over her hand. "Start at the beginning."

The beginning? She didn't want to go back there. "He got away."

Josh just stared at her.

"That means he'll kill again." She had to say those words. Her chest seemed to burn. "It's what he does, right?"

"*You* got away," Josh pointed out. "You're the first one, Casey. The only one who got away from this perp."

Because he'd killed the others. Dumped them in the ocean and hunted again. A shiver slid over her. "He said he'd been waiting for me."

Josh shot a quick glance at Hayden. The sheriff didn't speak.

"Is that what he always says?" Casey wondered. "Does he tell his victims that he's been waiting for them? Because he…he acted as if I were special, somehow. Like he'd been…he'd been trying to get me for a while." Nausea rose within her as she realized that, of course, they didn't know what he always said. As Josh had just told her…she was…

The only one who got away.

"Go back to the beginning," Hayden instructed her quietly. "I need to know everything about this guy."

She shivered. How was it so cold? "I was at my hotel. I'd just…I'd just gone inside after you dropped me off." She nodded toward Josh and his jaw hardened. "I went onto the balcony for a moment." Her gaze dropped to her feet. Her bare feet. "When I went back inside, the lights were off, and that was wrong because—" her head was pounding "—I'd turned on the light. It should have been on. I thought maybe there was a short, and I was going to call the front desk but…" Her gaze rose once more to meet Josh's. She swallowed the heavy lump that had risen in her throat. "He was already in the room. He grabbed me." Her fingers fluttered over her head. It was aching. Pounding. "He slammed me into the wall. At least twice, I think. I blacked out."

Josh swore, the words long and low and vicious.

"I don't remember how I got out here. I just woke up, and I was on the floor."

"I already sent a crime scene analysis team to your hotel," Josh said, his voice flat. "Maybe the guy left evidence behind that we can use."

The FBI and the local authorities were already working closely together, so she wasn't surprised that a team was already combing over her room. There was also a team at the scene there, going into the partially constructed houses, checking them one by one—starting with the house she'd been inside. Her chill got worse. "Do you think… Did he kill them all in that house?"

Josh and Hayden shared another hard look.

Maybe that look was answer enough.

"There was plastic on the floor," she whispered. "When I woke up, he had me in that upstairs room, tied up, and there was plastic beneath me." Just like a scene from a horror show.

"Are you *sure* you didn't see his face?" Josh pressed.

The pounding in her head grew worse. "He had on a ski mask. And the eyes—where the ski mask holes should have been, something like mesh covered his eyes so I couldn't see them. I didn't see his face. Didn't see his eyes, but I—I did see his hands." She eased out a slow breath. "He's Caucasian. Big—over six feet. Strong. Not heavy, but muscled." A killer in his prime. "His voice was rasping and low." Her body swayed as the nausea rolled within her again. For a moment, she thought she might vomit right then and there.

"Casey?" Josh's hand closed over her shoulder.

"She needs to get to a hospital!" The EMT was back. "The woman suffered head trauma. She needs medical attention and I am *insisting*, Sheriff, that you let her go."

Hayden nodded. "I'll talk to you again, Ms. Quinn."

Josh started to back away. She tensed and actually thought about grabbing him and *making* him stay with her.

But she didn't. Casey let him go. Josh jumped out of the ambulance. The EMT hurried back in to her side.

"You okay, miss?" he asked.

She was so far beyond okay.

Other reporters had already made it to the area. She saw Deputy Finn Patrick trying to hold some of them back so they didn't contaminate the crime scene. His dark hair was mussed and he appeared shaken. Cameras were rolling. Cameras that would focus on her.

I am the story.

Would her past come to light now? Probably. When the right people went digging, it was easy enough to find secrets.

But maybe…maybe someone already knew her secrets.

The man who'd taken her. The man who'd gotten away.

Josh stared at Casey a moment longer, then he slammed the ambulance doors shut. The siren screamed on.

Her eyes closed.

"You're safe now," the EMT assured her. Josh had pretty much said the same words.

But she wasn't so sure that she *was* safe.

I think he'll come after me again.

JOSH WATCHED THE ambulance drive away—the reporters had to clear a path so the vehicle could get by. The reporters were definitely already swarming the scene. Casey's story would be huge.

A survivor.

His hands fisted. He'd wanted to stay in that ambulance with her. "Make sure that a deputy remains with her at the hospital," he snapped to Hayden. "Someone needs to be with her every moment."

Hayden nodded. "Finn! Finn, get over here."

The young deputy rushed toward them. Sweat had already slickened the sides of his dark hair. "Sir?"

"Follow the ambulance. Make sure that Casey Quinn is guarded at all times."

Oh, hell, he was sending the kid after her? The deputy rushed to his patrol car, and Josh muttered, "You think that's the best plan? A woman survives a serial killer attack and gets the junior ranger for a guard?"

Hayden lifted a brow. "You got a problem with Finn?"

Yeah, he did.

"He's young, but he's good at his job. Protecting her will be his priority—"

"Sorry, Sheriff," Josh said curtly. "But the FBI has ranking jurisdiction here." The instant they'd confirmed the presence of a serial killer, the FBI had assumed control of the investigation. "And I'll be taking Casey Quinn into protective custody."

Hayden's eyes widened. "Will you now." Not a question, not really.

The ambulance was gone. And Josh didn't like having Casey out of his sight. There were some local

FBI agents on the scene and he knew he could leave them in the area to help with the search. "I'm going after her." *I should have been in the ambulance with her.*

"You think the killer will go after Casey Quinn again?"

"I don't know what he'll do, not yet. This is the first time one of his victims has gotten away." At least, the only victim they *knew* of escaping. "For all we know, he'll immediately go gunning for her again, and if that happens, I want more than just Deputy Patrick standing between her and danger." The kid was still green behind the ears.

"*You* want to be standing between her and the threat."

Josh's chin notched up. "She stabbed her attacker. I think that shows that she's capable of protecting herself... But her attack...it could very well have enraged the perp." *No doubt about that... My money says the guy is somewhere, choking on his rage.* "That means he could fixate on her. He could come at her with all he's got or..." His sentence trailed off.

"Or...?" Hayden prompted.

Josh glanced at the line of unfinished houses. "Or he will grab the next available victim who matches his profile. He'll let his rage out on her." Which meant they needed to be on guard—all of them.

"For someone who said he wasn't a profiler, you seem to know your killers pretty well."

He definitely wasn't a profiler. "I work on evidence collection. I don't poke into the heads of killers." His buddy Tucker did that. And Tucker Frost was scheduled to arrive in town any moment. The guy had just finished up a case in Colorado and now he was working on the profile for the killer in Hope. The FBI brass hadn't been satisfied with the work of the other profiler who'd been in town, and when Tucker finished his last case—he'd been immediately reassigned to Hope. When Tucker arrived, Josh knew the guy would want to speak with Casey right away. She would be key to the investigation.

"I have to make sure she doesn't say too much to the media." Another problem. Since she was a reporter, Casey would no doubt want to run live with her story. That wasn't going to happen.

He turned on his heel and headed for his motorcycle.

"Duvane!" Hayden's voice thundered after him.

He glanced over his shoulder. He liked Hayden—the guy was tough, smart and didn't generally take crap from anyone. But then again, Hayden was a former SEAL, and most folks knew better than to mess with SEALs.

"Is this personal?" Hayden asked him, voice quieter.

Personal?

Hayden eased toward him. "You dropped the reporter off at her hotel last night?"

Josh nodded.

Hayden's head cocked to the right. "Didn't realize you two knew each other so well."

They didn't know each other well. So his reaction

to her shouldn't be as intense as it was. But… "She's a victim. And my job is to protect victims." Lately, it seemed as if all he'd done had been to discover the dead. Casey wasn't dead, and he damn well wasn't going to let anything else happen to her.

Hayden's stare was assessing. "Better watch yourself. Once emotions get involved, the cases become even harder." His lips twisted in a humorless smile. "Trust me—I know exactly what I'm talking about."

Josh knew the guy was speaking from experience because the woman Hayden loved, Jill West, had been targeted by Theodore Anderson. Theodore had first kidnapped Jill when she was just a kid, but Jill had managed to escape him. Years later, she'd returned to Hope, determined to finally solve the mystery of her past. But her return had set off a deadly chain of reactions… In the end, Jill and Hayden had both been fighting for their lives.

They'd won, though. They'd stopped the killer. They'd unmasked Theodore Anderson. And now Jill and Hayden were finally free to work on their future together.

But Josh *wasn't* Hayden, and Casey…she wasn't Jill. They didn't have a past that linked them, and as far as how he felt about her… "Emotions aren't an issue for me. She's just a case." Simple words. Emotions didn't get to him. He did his job, and he moved on. Simple.

"Keep telling yourself that," Hayden mumbled.

Josh climbed onto the motorcycle. He glanced

over at the house and saw the yellow line of crime scene tape.

Casey could have died in that house.

His jaw clenched. The killer wouldn't get close to her again. Not on his watch.

SHE'D BEEN POKED and prodded for hours. *Hours.* And Casey was not a happy woman. Her control was barely holding on, and any moment, she was afraid she might just break apart.

She didn't want to break in front of the too friendly nurses. Or the steely-eyed doctors. Or *anyone.*

"Are we done yet?" Casey asked, fighting to keep her voice calm.

Dr. Abernathy, a young African American woman with small, wire-framed glasses and a no-nonsense manner, looked up from Casey's charts. "You are a very lucky woman, Ms. Quinn."

She had to swallow three times before she could manage to speak again. "Luckier than the other victims."

A faint furrow appeared between the doctor's eyes.

"I don't feel sick any longer. I don't have the headache—"

"It's good that you're feeling better, but I'd like to keep you for observation a bit longer. You took a severe blow to the head—"

"I just told you my head felt fine now." Only a tiny lie. Her head still ached a bit, but it was nothing she couldn't handle.

"In concussion cases, the victim may suffer from seizures or convulsions. It's possible that you could become confused and agitated—"

"I feel plenty agitated right now," Casey muttered as she fiddled with the paper hospital gown that she was wearing. Her clothes had been taken, confiscated as evidence by the authorities. "Thank you for all that you've done. Really, thank you. But I want to get out of here, okay? I don't have nausea, no blurred vision, no memory lapses. I know our president. I know my birthday. I know—"

The curtain on the side of her bed swung back. "You know that you're causing trouble."

Her breath left in a quick rush. Josh. "I—I thought you were at the crime scene." She pulled up her covers—or rather, the thin sheet that was her only cover, other than the paper gown. "How long have you been here?" Had he just been hanging around, eavesdropping on her talk with the doctor? Didn't he get there was a whole patient privacy issue going on?

He stepped closer to the bed. A line of stubble coated his hard jaw. "Been here long enough to know that you're pushing yourself too hard."

"No, I'm not. I let the doctors check me out. I did everything they wanted." Her shoulders straightened. "Now, I *want* to go back to my hotel—" But even as she said the words, she stopped. No, she didn't want to go back to the hotel. She didn't want to return to that dark room and remember what it had been like when the attacker grabbed her.

"Your room isn't an option."

Because a crime scene team was still there? "I'm sure I can get another hotel room."

His jaw hardened. "What you're getting is a safe house."

A what?

"Um, excuse me," the doctor began.

Josh flashed his ID at her. "FBI. I'm Josh Duvane, and I'll be seeing to Ms. Quinn's security."

"I told you to call me Casey," she reminded him, again.

He flashed her a hard look.

Fine. Enough of this. Casey shoved back her thin cover. If need be, she'd leave that place in her paper gown. She swung her legs over the side of the bed. She started to rise—

Josh locked his hands around her shoulders and pushed her back down. "You aren't going anywhere."

Her eyes narrowed on him. "Yes, *I* am going someplace. I'm getting out of here. Because I don't like hospitals. I don't like getting poked and prodded, and since nothing is wrong with me, there's no reason I can't just walk right out of that door."

There was more to it than that. She had a very specific reason for not liking hospitals. Once, she'd spent far too much time in a hospital. She'd grown to hate those white walls and the scent of antiseptic. That scent was like death to her.

He glanced at the doctor.

"She needs someone to stay with her," Dr. Abernathy said. "In case she has any issues—blurred vision, slurred speech, convulsions…"

Oh, yes, that lovely list again. "I'll bunk with my camerawoman. Katrina can make sure I'm okay." Speaking of Katrina, the woman was probably freaking out. Casey needed to talk with her immediately but no one had let her have a phone.

Not helpful.

"If I make sure she isn't alone," Josh said, his hands still around her shoulders, "will she be able to leave?"

Dr. Abernathy nodded. "Yes, but if she displays any of those symptoms, she has to return to the hospital right away."

He nodded. "Done."

Done?

"I'll get an orderly to help Ms. Quinn to the car," Dr. Abernathy stated briskly. "Patient pickup is located at the front side of the building—"

"And that side is covered by reporters. I'll be getting Casey out, don't worry about that."

The doctor blinked. "Uh, right. Okay, then. I'll go prepare the discharge paperwork." She exited the room. Josh didn't move.

Casey stared up at him. "Safe house?"

"Yes, it's a place we put victims or potential witnesses so we can be sure that—"

"I *know* what a safe house is," she said. "But since when am I going to one?"

"Since you escaped a killer?"

"Josh—"

"I'm afraid you're being taken into protective custody for the time being." His hands slid away from her. He turned and paced toward the door—and he picked up a small duffel bag that she hadn't even noticed before. "And while you're under protective custody, I have to ask that you refrain from speaking with reporters."

"I *am* a reporter."

He brought the bag to her. She glanced inside and relief filled her. Clothes. The guy had stopped and picked up some of her clothes. "I could kiss you," she mumbled.

"If you want…"

Her gaze jerked up to his.

He stared at her. The tension between them mounted. She hadn't even been thinking when she'd spoken. It had just been an expression but now…

She swallowed. "You're not…you're not like other FBI agents, are you?"

"You've met a lot of us?"

"My fair share." She felt too exposed. Being in front of him, just that thin gown covering her skin, made her feel too vulnerable. "Side effect of my job, you know? I tend to cross paths with the authorities a lot." She was rambling. Casey clamped her lips shut.

His hand lifted and he touched her cheek.

Casey flinched.

"Easy…"

"There is nothing easy about how I feel right now." Her whole life was out of control.

His gaze was on her cheek. "Does it hurt?"

"The cut or the bruise?" Then she shook her head. "Doesn't matter. Josh, get me *out* of here."

"It matters." His voice was rough, his gaze gleaming. "It matters one hell of a lot to me." He stepped away. "Do you need help changing?"

Help… Ah, him? Seeing her naked? "No, I…have it."

He pulled the curtain back into place.

"You're just…standing there?" On the other side of that thin curtain?

"I can't see you."

She slid off the bed and dressed—slowly. She didn't want to fall and have him rushing back in to pick her nearly naked self off the floor. After sliding into the underwear and bra, she put on jeans and pulled on a T-shirt. He'd even brought her some tennis shoes. He'd covered all the bases. What a guy.

"Casey?"

She left the gown on the bed. "I'm done."

He shoved back the curtain. His gaze raked her.

Her hands twisted. "So…a safe house, huh?" Crap. She'd said that before. "Just how long will I be staying there?"

He caught one of her twisting hands in his and led her to the door. "I don't know yet."

That wasn't good. Not knowing implied it could be days. Weeks? No, absolutely not. She had a job. She had a story to cover.

I am the story. Her stomach twisted.

"Who'll be staying with me?" They were walking down the polished hallway of the hospital. He kept his grip on her hand and he stayed firmly at her side.

He'd probably drop her at the safe house and vanish. After all, his work was in the water—

"For the time being, I am."

She stopped. "You. But…why?"

He turned toward her. His gaze wasn't gleaming now. It was burning with emotion that she couldn't read. "Because I *can* keep you safe. No threat will come to you when I'm near."

She wanted to believe him. He sounded so confident, and right then, she was feeling…scared. Casey didn't let herself fear much, but after her night from hell? She figured she was entitled to some good, old-fashioned terror.

He was going to kill me.

"You fought him off. You survived." Josh's voice was so deep and dark. "Now my job is to make sure you *keep* surviving."

"But…I thought you were the USERT lead—"

"I am, and I'll keep working with USERT. But right now, I don't have a body to search for."

Because she'd survived.

He started walking again. He stopped near the elevator and pressed the button to bring it up. A moment later, the door dinged. They stepped inside, and he hit the button to take them down to the basement. No, to the parking garage.

When the doors closed, they seemed to immediately be wrapped in intimacy. Why did the elevator feel so small? Or maybe he just seemed too big.

"Are we using your motorcycle?" Casey bit her lip. "Because I'd really prefer a different ride."

His lips quirked. "Already ahead of you. Got a rental waiting for us."

Again, he'd covered all the bases. He must have been a Boy Scout back in the day.

"When we get to the safe house, another agent will be waiting for us. He's going to need to hear your story again."

The doors dinged open. The parking garage waited. She started to step out, but Josh caught her arm and pulled her back. Then *he* went out first, and his gaze swept the scene.

"You really think he's coming after me again, don't you?"

He kept a tight hold on her arm as he led her to a dark SUV. His rental. He put her in the passenger side and didn't speak until he'd slid in behind the steering wheel. He locked the doors, turned on the engine then glanced over at her. His gaze was hooded as he said, "I think we have two options with a killer like him."

A serial killer. A sadistic—

"You're the first victim—that we know of—who has gotten away. He may look at you as unfinished business. He may focus on you. Fixate."

That sounded very, very *not* good.

"Or he may immediately pick a new victim to replace you."

Someone to die while she lived? Casey shook her

head. "I don't like either option." Her voice came out sounding very small.

"Neither do I." He drove them out of the garage. She looked to the side as they left the hospital, and saw plenty of familiar faces in the crowd of reporters. "That's why Hayden has his men and the local Bureau agents combing this town. We have to find the perp before anyone else is hurt."

Before he attacked someone else...

Or before he comes for me again.

I SEE YOU, CASEY.

He stood at the back of the pack of reporters. They were all staring at the main entrance to the hospital, hoping to get a glimpse of Casey Quinn. One of their own had just become the center of their attention.

But they should have focused their attention elsewhere. He'd been glancing toward the parking garage exit, and he'd just seen the SUV slip away. For a moment, Casey had glanced back, almost seeming to look right at him. She'd been in the passenger seat, and her hand had risen to press against the window.

I see you.

He noted the license plate for that vehicle. He hadn't been able to glimpse the driver, but with all the Feds running around town, he was betting Casey had just gotten herself some protection. Not that protection would do her any good.

He eased away from the crowd and slipped into his car. The dark SUV—Casey's getaway SUV—was stopped at a red light just ahead. Simple enough to spot. Easy enough to follow.

He'd just see where Casey was going because he wasn't done with her. Not by a long shot.

He and Casey were just getting started.

Chapter Five

She had a bruise on her cheek and fear in her eyes. Josh didn't like that—didn't like the bruise, didn't like the small cut on top of the bruise and he didn't like the way her body trembled as she walked into the safe house that he'd secured for her. They'd traveled to the newest condominium complex in Hope and they were in the penthouse unit, a unit that provided them with maximum security. There were video cameras positioned in the hallway, and a guard stationed to review IDs in the lobby.

He'd checked out the small town of Hope and figured this place was Casey's best bet. It was the most secure building in the area.

"The place has a killer view," Casey murmured. She stood in front of the floor-to-ceiling windows that overlooked the beach. Her arms were wrapped around her stomach. She glanced back at him and raised her brows. "The FBI must be spending a ton of money on me."

He strode toward her. Her scent—light, and still

reminding him of candy—drifted to him. "Don't worry about the money." Her safety was what mattered.

"I thought you said there was going to be another FBI agent here."

"Tucker will be arriving any moment." He'd gotten a text from Tucker right when they arrived. The other agent had been delayed because he had to meet with Hayden. Special Agent Tucker Frost was the behavioral specialist who'd been sent to figure out the killer—and to replace the guy who hadn't made any progress on the case for the past three weeks. FBI brass had wanted a change, a fresh perspective—so Tucker had been shipped down to Florida. "There's a new…team working within the FBI," he said. "Tucker is part of that team."

Her head cocked.

"A few agents have been hand selected for this group. Their job is to specifically track and apprehend serials." He was being very careful with what he shared—after all, Casey was a reporter.

"And you didn't want to be part of this group?" She turned away from the windows and focused completely on him. Her arms were still around her stomach, as if she were trying to warm herself. Or shield herself.

He took another step toward her even as he gave a slow shake of his head. "I don't like climbing into a killer's mind." That wasn't for him. Figuring out what made those monsters tick? Looking into the darkness and having it try to swallow you whole? No, he'd come too close to that before. "I work with the victims."

Her lips parted. "You bring them home."

"I find them…and I find the evidence we need to lock the killers away. That's the job I like—making sure that no one gets away with murder."

She studied him a moment, seeming to consider his words, then she said, "I—I should call my boss, Tom. I should talk to Katrina, too. Let them know what happened. They must be worried sick about me."

Her voice had softened a bit when she mentioned her boss's name. "I already contacted Katrina and told her you were all right. She said she was calling your producer."

"That's Tom. Tom Warren. He's the producer of the show—and the guy pretty much controls *everything* that happens on the show. He'll want to talk to me." Her hands dropped. "I don't have my phone, though. When I was, um, taken from the hotel room, I didn't exactly get a chance to grab it and—"

His hands closed around her shoulders. "Stop." Because her words were too brittle. Her expression too guarded. "You're safe, Casey. Do you hear me? *Safe.* I'm not going to let anyone hurt you."

And…he saw the change in her expression. The

fear that couldn't be denied as it swept over her face. "I've heard that promise before."

What?

"It wasn't true then." Tears gleamed in her eyes but she blinked quickly, not letting those tears fall. "And I'm scared it won't be true now."

What was she talking about? "You were attacked before?" The rage he'd tried to control grew like a fire in his blood. "Casey, what in the hell—"

She jerked away from him and her eyes had flashed wide. "It's going to come back, isn't it? *I'm the story…*just like I thought, and it will all come back again." She frantically shook her head, then her hand rose to press to her temple. "I didn't want it back. I worked too hard to bury the truth."

He caught her fingers in his hand. "Casey."

She blinked at him.

"What truth?" The gnawing in his gut told him this was bad.

"I should call Katrina," she said again. "Just to check in. I don't have any family members who will worry, but I need to tell her—"

His hold tightened on her hand. "She knows you're okay. But I'll make sure you talk to her, okay? Right after we finish with Tucker, you can call her."

She pulled in a deep breath. "Thank you."

His chest felt too tight. "Casey—"

But there was a sharp knock at the door. She stiffened, and he wanted to pull her against him. Wanted to hold her tight and tell her that everything was all right.

It wasn't all right, though. Not with the killer still out there.

"Stay here." He headed for the door, and his gaze swept to the laptop he'd opened on the table near the entrance. He'd already set up a feed so that he could see the security cameras in the building. There were four images displayed on his screen, and in one of those images, he saw a man standing just outside the penthouse.

The guy turned toward the camera and inclined his dark head.

"Tucker." Josh unlocked the door and offered his hand to the other agent. "Good to see you again."

Tucker's shake was firm. "Wish it were under better circumstances." His bright blue stare held Josh's. "I've got a key to the place, but I thought the vic might appreciate a heads-up before I came in."

Josh heard the faint tread of footsteps behind him. "The *vic*," Casey said, her voice flat and her emotions once more seemingly locked down, "has a name."

Tucker's brows climbed. "Casey Quinn, I presume."

Josh backed away so that Tucker could march past him. Josh shut and locked the door and his gaze swept to the security feed. No other activity.

Tucker offered his hand to Casey. "I'm FBI Special Agent Tucker Frost."

She backed up a step and didn't take his offered hand. "Frost." Casey seemed to taste the name, and Josh knew it instantly clicked for her when her gaze sharpened. "I remember you…and your brother." Her head cocked and then her hand was rising. Her delicate fingers were swallowed by Tucker's much bigger hand. "I'm sorry."

"Sorry?" Tucker murmured. He didn't let her hand go. "That's not the response most people have to me—or to my brother."

"I'm not most people."

The guy could let go of her hand at any point. Josh cleared his throat. They were just standing there, staring at each other. "Casey's been through a hell of a lot—why don't we let her sit down while she tells you what happened? The doc warned me to keep an eye on her."

Tucker finally let go of her hand. About time, Josh figured. Concern shadowed Tucker's eyes as his gaze swept over her. "I'm sorry about the attack." His fingers lifted to brush her cheek. "Are you—"

Josh pulled Casey back. "No, she's not okay. She's not going to be okay until we catch the jerk who's out there." He normally liked Tucker. The guy was a good agent. But right then…

I'm jealous. The emotion caught him by surprise. He was never jealous—and he and Casey had just met. She was a witness. A victim. Nothing more.

Maybe I just feel protective of her. Maybe that's it.

He steered her toward the couch. She sat down,

but didn't relax. Instead, Casey perched on the edge of the sofa.

Tucker looked at her, then at Josh. "Something I need to know about?"

"Yeah." Josh kept standing at her side. "You need to know about the freak who came into her hotel room, knocked her out and dragged her away to kill her. Let's focus on him for a bit." The anger in him was getting worse. Josh raked a hand through his hair. "Because he's still out there. I need something to guide the team toward him. We need to *stop* him because he got away clean at the scene."

"Not completely clean," Casey said, her voice husky. "I stabbed him. He was coming at me, and I had to stop him."

Right. She'd told him that back at the beach house. "The evidence unit collected the blade—they'll be running checks on the blood. Maybe we'll get a hit on him in the system."

"You stabbed him?" Admiration deepened Tucker's voice. "I'm impressed."

"I wasn't going to die in that room. He'd set the stage, but that wasn't how things were going to end for me." Her hands fisted in her lap. "Where do you want me to start? When I woke up on the plastic or—"

"Your hotel room." Tucker sat down next to her. "Start there. Tell me everything you remember, big and small. Those pieces will help me to understand the man we're after."

They already did understand him, to a certain degree. They were after what the behavioral analysts called an "organized" killer—a killer who carefully planned his crimes. Who didn't leave evidence behind. Casey had already told Josh that the man had worn gloves and a mask to cover his face. He'd had the plastic spread out beneath her—a clever touch—so that the scene would be easy to contain.

She let out a low sigh. "I was on my balcony and when I turned to go back inside, I noticed that the lights were out. I—I'd left one light on before I went outside—"

"You're sure about that?" Tucker broke in.

"Yes." Her voice was certain. "But I just thought maybe the bulb had blown or there was a problem with the fuse. Something like that. I was going to call the front desk when he grabbed me and slammed my head into the wall."

"How did he grab you?" Tucker asked.

She swallowed. "From behind. I didn't even see him, didn't hear him. He was suddenly just there and he shoved me forward into the wall."

The fury was still thickening in Josh's blood. "You told me you heard his laughter."

She glanced toward him. "I did. I remember him laughing right before I passed out."

His muscles were tight, his body thick with tension.

"When I woke up, my hands were tied behind me and my feet were tied." Her gaze slid back to Tucker.

"I was lying on the plastic, and I could smell the ocean. I could hear it. There was just enough light for me to see the room around me, and I realized I was in one of the houses under construction. Katrina and I had recorded some footage near them just the week before." She licked her lips. Once more, her gaze darted to Josh. "Did he kill them all in that beach house?"

"The techs used luminol and found traces of latent blood." So, yes…he thought the other victims had been killed there but it would be a while before they received any sort of conclusive results on the blood evidence that had been collected at the scene. The homes under construction were isolated, and on the weekend, no workers came out to them. It would have been an ideal spot for a killer and his victim. "We'll know more once we get additional reports." Once the samples collected had been compared to their victims. "There wasn't a lot of blood found. The guy was probably trying to keep the scene clean with his plastic, but with these kinds of attacks, there can be a great deal of—" He stopped, hating to say more.

"Blood spatter?" Casey asked softly. "Yes, I know."

Of course, she would. Casey wasn't an ordinary civilian. So why was he treating her with kid gloves?

Because she's wounded. She's fragile. She's frightened.

She's…different. Something about her was calling to him.

"Where was he, when you woke up?" Tucker asked.

"Outside the room. I didn't see him at all and I screamed for help." Her breath whispered out. "My scream brought him to me."

"Describe every detail of him that you remember." Tucker was focused completely on her. He'd taken his laptop from his bag and he had it open in his lap as he listened to her.

"He was…tall, like you and Josh. Probably almost the same height, I would guess a little over six feet. Muscled. Broad shoulders." Again, she nodded toward Josh. "He had on a ski mask with some kind of mesh over the eyes, so I don't know his eye color. I can't describe his face. But he was Caucasian, I know that. He was wearing gloves, but I saw his wrist. It was tanned, like he'd spent time outdoors."

The town of Hope was right on the beach. Nearly every Caucasian male in the area was sporting at least a light tan.

"When he came in…he said he'd heard me scream-ing. And that meant it was time to *get started*."

Bastard. "Did he have any accent?" Josh demanded. "Did anything about his voice stand out to you?"

She shook her head. "He was…rasping. I don't think that was his normal voice."

Tucker shot Josh a fast, hard glance. Josh nodded. *The guy is hiding his identity. Odd, since he planned to kill Casey. Usually when the perps think there is no hope for their prey, they'll show their faces.*

But this time…

"He…he said I was going to tell him all of my secrets." She licked her lips. "And that if I didn't, he would cut me open."

Josh surged away from the couch. *I will find you. I will make you pay.*

"I don't think…he expected me to fight back. I mean, I was tied up, so maybe he thought I'd be helpless. Or too afraid to fight back. But I wasn't going to die there."

She's strong. Strong and brave. He locked his legs and stared down at her.

"I kicked him with my bound feet. He fell back and lost his knife. I got it and used it on the ropes around my wrists, but he hit me before I could get free." Her hand rose to her dark cheek.

He will pay.

"H-he said he had to do step one."

Silence. Josh's heavy heartbeat drummed in his ears.

"What was step one?" Tucker asked.

"Making a phone call. To Sheriff Black. The guy said…he said we had to let people know who had the power." Her hand fell back to her lap. "But the sheriff wanted proof of life, and when the guy in the mask turned back to me—I think he was going to try to make me scream—I shouted at the sheriff, telling him where I thought I was. I was hoping he'd come for me in time."

Josh rolled back his shoulders. Casey had told him this story before, at the crime scene. She'd told him how, after the phone call, she'd stabbed the attacker. He'd fled and she'd been left alone in that house.

"I forgot." Her voice was low. "I forgot what he said…"

Josh stalked toward her.

Her head snapped up and she stared straight at him. "I didn't tell you before… I forgot…but he said, *I've waited too long to get you, Casey.* Those were his words. As if he'd always intended to take me."

Tucker had gone still beside her.

"But he was just talking, just scaring me, right?" Her gaze swung between the two men. "I mean, he picked me after his last victim was dead. It's not like the guy has been after me for a long time or anything."

The killings started after all the reporters came to town to cover Theodore Anderson's case and sentencing.

"Josh?" She rose to her feet and came toward him. "He hasn't been after me for a long time. I was just— just his next victim, right? Like you said, I fit the victim profile. Right age, right sex. From out of town. No close ties here…"

Tucker cleared his throat when Josh remained silent. "There could be more to our profile," he said carefully. "It changes and adjusts as we gather additional information about our perp."

She was standing in front of Josh. Her body trembled. He'd never forget seeing her in that beach house, holding that bloody knife.

"Was there anything about him that seemed familiar to you?" Josh asked her because the knot in his stomach told him where Tucker's profile was heading. He didn't like getting into the heads of killers but in this case…with her…*for* her, he'd do it.

"Familiar?" Her laughter was bitter. "No, a man in a black ski mask who wants to cut me up and learn my secrets isn't exactly familiar to me."

Tucker had risen, too. "Since you've been in town, have you been seeing anyone romantically, started dating any locals or any other reporters or—"

She didn't look away from Josh. "I'm not dating anyone."

"What about in the past…maybe when you were in New York?" Tucker added. "Could you give us a list of the men you were seeing back home?"

Her chin notched up. "You want a list of my lovers, is that what you're saying?"

Tucker cleared his throat. "I think that might be helpful, yes."

Her eyes were on Josh. "Because you think one of them—one of the men I've slept with in the past— came all the way down here, killed three other women, dumped their bodies in the ocean and then came after *me*. That's what you think?"

Josh wanted to touch her. To smooth away the

line between her brows. "Based on what he said, it seems that this perp was focusing on you, Casey. By looking at those close to you, we may be able to find out why."

"Maybe he said the same thing to every woman he took." Now she glanced over at Tucker. "That's what killers like him do, right? They follow their rituals, their rules. Like step one...calling the sheriff—taunting him. Then step two...was learning the secrets of his victims. Maybe he said the same crap to us all. There's nothing personal there between us. I don't know him."

"He had on a mask," Tucker pointed out. "And you said he even disguised his voice. Maybe you *do* know him. And...you're a celebrity, Casey. Even if you don't personally know him, he may feel that he knows you. You're on his TV every week. That could have led to a fixation. It could have led—"

"To him kidnapping me and trying to kill me? To killing all of those other women?"

Tucker just stared at her. "I'll need the names of your lovers, ma'am. I need the names of any close friends you have down here *and* back in New York. On a case like this, every angle must be explored."

Her cheeks had flushed a dark pink. "The list is short, okay? I haven't had a boyfriend in two years, so there isn't anyone back home who needs to make your list. As far as friends—yes, I have a lot of those, but they're mostly superficial. I don't exactly let a lot of people close." She exhaled. "But I'll still make you the list. I just… Can I rest first? My head is aching again and I just—I need a minute." She brushed past Josh.

No, she *tried* to brush past him. He caught her arms and forced her to look at him. "You okay?"

Her laugh sounded bitter and rough. "I am very far from okay." Her eyes were filled with moisture but, just like before, she blinked before any teardrops could fall. "Where's my room?"

"Down the hallway. Second door on the right." His was the first door. He let her go. Josh watched as she hurried down the hallway and slipped into the second room on the right. When the door closed behind her, he turned back to focus on Tucker.

Tucker Frost. Like Josh, the guy had a dangerous past. When it came to killers, things were very, very personal for Tucker. No wonder his name had clicked for Casey. Being a reporter, there would have been no way for her to miss the sensational story that had been Tucker's life, even if that bloody hell had made the news years ago. Some stories were never forgotten.

"She has secrets," Josh said flatly. For some reason, when he said those words, he felt as if he were almost betraying her. Ridiculous, of course. He was just doing his job. But…

Tucker lifted a brow. "You seem to be very close to our victim."

She's more than a victim. "I'm the one who took her to the hotel right before she was abducted." *I'm the one who will never leave her alone like that again.*

"And here I thought Ms. Quinn said she didn't have a lover in the area."

He took a step toward the other agent, but caught himself. "*Not* like that," he gritted out. He'd known Tucker for a long time…way before they'd joined the FBI. Back when they'd been two lost men trying to save the world, one bloody battle at a time. Tucker had been the one to actually convince him to join the FBI. Tucker had been the one to tell him that there was a place for Josh at the Bureau.

Tucker had wanted to focus on the killers. He'd been obsessed with finding out how to get in their heads. With Tucker's past, Josh certainly understood why. But…

For me, it's always been about the victims.

"She was waiting outside the sheriff's station. I gave her a ride back to her place. That is *all*."

Tucker rolled back his shoulders. "Then how do you know about the secrets?"

"I can tell when a woman is hiding something. She admitted it herself—no close friends, no lovers that she lets in. She's protecting herself."

"Which one of us is building the profile?" Tucker mused.

Josh raked a hand through his hair. "You know I don't go for that. I don't want in their heads." Too much darkness lived there. Once, the darkness had tried to swallow him alive. After a mission gone horribly wrong. "I'm going to dig into her past. I'll find out what she's hiding."

"Her past could be tied to the killer."

That was what he feared. "We both know that two killers of this caliber—Theodore Anderson and the perp who attacked her—there is no way they should both have been hunting in this town." The odds were just against that ever occurring.

Only it *had* occurred.

"We need to talk with Theodore Anderson," Tucker said. The faint lines near his mouth deepened. "Right now, Sheriff Black is operating under the assumption that Anderson committed his crimes alone. But maybe that's not the case. Maybe there was always someone else in the background."

Josh swore. "Someone who isn't content to stay in the background any longer? Not with Anderson out of the way?" When Anderson's sentencing had come down a few weeks ago, everyone had known that the man would never step foot outside those prison walls.

Tucker nodded. "That's one possibility. Option two…" His gaze slid toward the hallway. "Option two is that this killer was drawn to this town. Drawn to the crowd of reporters and the attention that Anderson received. He wanted his own spotlight so—"

"What better way to get in the spotlight than by

taking a star reporter?" Talk about a victim that would grab headlines.

His friend exhaled. "Then we have our third option. It's the one I like least of all."

Josh knew this option. It was—

"Personal," Tucker said. "The killer went after Casey Quinn specifically. He targeted the other women, but only because he was working up to her. If he hadn't ever killed before these attacks in Hope, then he would have wanted to perfect his craft before getting to his real goal. His main prey."

And that prey? It could be Casey.

Chapter Six

"Are you sure you're all right?" Katrina demanded, her sharp voice showing her worry. "I mean…the killer took you, Casey. He *took* you."

Her hold tightened on the phone. Josh had brought the phone to her a few moments before, and then he'd urged her to be very, very careful with the facts she shared with her friend. He'd also told Casey that she wouldn't be getting her own phone back anytime soon—it had been bagged as evidence at her hotel.

As soon as he'd slipped out to go and join his FBI buddy again, she'd been calling Katrina. "I'm okay. I promise. Nothing that won't heal."

"Where are you? The FBI has been giving me some bull story about you being in protective custody—"

"It's not bull." She turned and glanced at the closed door. "I'm in a safe house, for the moment."

"What?"

That cry nearly split Casey's eardrum. "It's just temporary, okay? Agent Duvane got me out of the hospital and brought me here so I could rest. I think my hotel room is still crime scene central—"

"Tom moved us out of that hotel," Katrina said quickly. "We all have rooms at a new place. Way better security, I promise. So you don't need to stay with the FBI. You can come over here. Tom is right next door, and seriously, the guy is about to go out of his head. He wants to talk to you. You know, I don't think he's over that crush he had on you—"

"Tom doesn't have a crush on me. Tom just wants a story. A big story. Having his reporter escape death is going to give him huge ratings, and he knows it." Ratings on TV. Hits on the web. Everything a producer could desire. "But tell him he has to wait. The FBI said I couldn't talk to the media yet."

"You *are* the media."

"And I'm the victim." She dropped onto the edge of the bed. The mattress sagged a bit beneath her. "They've got me talking to some kind of profiler now." Though profiler wouldn't be his technical term. Profilers didn't actually exist in the FBI. The guy—Tucker Frost—she figured he was working for the Behavioral Analysis Unit.

A man who understood killers.

With what she knew of Tucker's past, she figured he would understand them very, very well.

"Is that her?" A man's voice sounded in the background and she knew Tom had come into Katrina's room. Not surprising, really, since she knew Katrina

and Tom hooked up frequently. *And yet another reason why the man is not interested in me at all.*

"Let me talk to Casey," Tom continued.

Casey's heels kicked against the side of the bed as she swung her feet and waited.

"Casey," his deep voice boomed over the line. "Tell me where you are and I will come get you right now."

"That's not an option, Tom. I'm at a safe house. Places like this stay safe because you don't tell people where they are."

"Casey...you're the lead story on every television in the US right now. You have to give me something. Tell me about the man who took you. Tell me what he looked like. What he said. Tell me—"

Her bedroom door opened. Josh seemed to fill the doorway.

"Casey?" Tom called in her ear. "Say something! I need *something*—"

"I'm okay, Tom. I survived." Her words sounded brittle even to her own ears. "Thanks for worrying."

"Wait, I *do* worry, I—"

Josh closed the door behind him and paced toward her. "End the call, Casey."

Had he been eavesdropping on her? That was such a terrible habit. She couldn't look away from him. "Got to go, Tom. I'll check in again soon."

"But I need a quote—"

Her fingers swiped over the screen, ending the call. Josh stood just over her. His gaze seemed hooded as he stared at her. She tipped back her head, looking up at him. "Don't worry, I didn't tell Tom or Katrina anything about this place." She glanced around the room. "I left out the fact that I was staying in the lap of luxury." She tossed the phone onto the bed beside her. "I just assured my friends that I was still in the land of the living."

His jaw hardened. "How's the head?"

"It—" She started to lie and say that it was perfectly fine, but there was just something about his gaze. So deep and dark. "It aches."

His hand lifted and his fingers feathered over her temple. "You should have stayed in the hospital."

She immediately tensed. "No, that was the last place I wanted to be."

He studied her a moment in silence, then turned on his heel and headed into the bathroom. A moment later, he was back, carrying a cloth that he put to her forehead, then swept over her temple. It was a cool, soft cloth, and it immediately made her feel better.

"Any blurred vision? Nausea?"

"Nothing. Just an aching head…because it collided too hard with a wall."

He slid the cloth over her temple again in a gentle caress. "I—I didn't expect gentleness from you."

"What did you expect?"

"Danger. Arrogance. Maybe some adrenaline-junkie personality traits."

"Just because I was a SEAL, it doesn't mean I was addicted to the high of battle."

No, it didn't. "Why were you a SEAL?"

He still towered over her, but, after a moment of silence, Josh moved to sit on the bed beside her, and suddenly, it was harder to breathe. Maybe because every breath brought her his rich, masculine scent.

"My father was a navy man, spent his whole life serving. When I was a kid, I bounced around, living all over the world as we headed to new bases. My mom and I—she always said it was an adventure. I liked that adventure."

Wanderlust…that was why he'd been a SEAL? No, she didn't buy it. "There's more to your story."

His lips twisted in a faint smile. "Going to feature me on your show? Trying to figure me out?"

"Not everything is about the show." She pushed away the cloth and her fingers tangled with his. Whenever they touched, she felt that contact straight to her soul. Crazy. Ridiculous. Just a product of her overwrought emotions.

Except…even before her attack, when he'd taken her on that motorcycle ride, his touch had burned straight to her soul.

"You want to know about me?" His faint smile stayed in place. "Well, I want to know about you, Casey Quinn. How about we trade secrets? I'll tell you my past, and you tell me yours."

Her hand lowered. Their fingers stayed intertwined. She couldn't look away from the sight of them. "You're going to dig into my past, anyway. You think I don't know that? Your buddy Tucker is probably already calling the FBI. He's telling them to pull up every single file they can find on Cassandra, AKA Casey, Quinn." She leaned toward him, putting her lips right next to his ear. "But here's the first secret, Josh. He won't find anything on Casey." Her lips brushed his ear. A deliberate move on her part. She was feeling too much—and her normal control wasn't in place. She was playing a dangerous game with him because playing made her feel alive. And she wanted to be alive.

She'd come too close to death.

"Why not? Why won't we find you?"

Was it her imagination or had his voice gone deeper? Darker?

"Because Casey Quinn didn't exist until seven years ago." When she'd turned eighteen, Casey had been born. Once more, her lips brushed against his ear. "I'm not real." Her secret, the truth she held so close, but she knew he'd find out. And it almost felt good to have her cards on the table. To not pretend, for once.

"If you're not Casey—" his voice was a little more than a growl now "—then who are you?"

Her heart ached as she trailed her finger down the column of his neck. "I'm the girl who should have died. Everyone else died, but I didn't."

His head turned toward her. His gaze blazed. "Casey—"

"Your turn." She had to force those words out. "No more from me. Tell me a truth, and don't say you're a former SEAL because you liked traveling to new places. I won't buy that. Do better."

"Fine." The word was nearly a snarl. "I'm good at hunting. A damn deadly weapon."

She shook her head. "Lie."

His eyes widened. "What?"

"Oh, I don't doubt that you're very good at hunting, and I'm sure you're a perfectly timed killing machine when the need arises, but that's still not the reason you were a SEAL." Her heart pounded hard in her chest. "Have I told you…I'm good at seeing lies? You can see lies in the way a person's eyes change." Her hand lifted and her fingers feathered near the corner of his eye. "When you look away from me or when you focus just beyond my gaze…dead give-away." Her hand dropped to his chest. "When your breath comes faster, when your heart pounds…I can see the lie. I've interviewed hundreds of witnesses in my time. I *had* to know who was telling me the truth, and who was just trying to lie to me."

"I'm a federal agent. I *know* how to control my responses. You don't see anything when I lie—"

"Got you," she whispered.

A furrow appeared between his heavy brows.

"You just confessed. You are lying. And here I was, telling you the truth." Disappointment rushed through her. "If this is going to work, I need you to be honest with me."

He edged ever closer to her. "And you'll be honest with me?"

She had been, so far.

"I wanted to make a difference. Be all I could be...just like my old man. When I got out there in the field, I found out that I did like the job. I liked the rush. But I was away on a mission when my mother *and* my father both died in a robbery. Some jerk held them up at gunpoint, stole one hundred dollars from my father. *One hundred dollars.* Like that's worth someone's life. He shot my father, and he shot my mother, and when I came home, all I had waiting for me were two coffins."

Her hand wrapped around his. "I'm sorry."

"Tucker is the one who came to me then. Telling me my skills could be put to use. Telling me there was a way to help right here at home. My family was gone, and I didn't want to ship out again. So I listened. I became part of the FBI and found my way to USERT." His lips twisted. "The water has always been part of me, so using my skills there again, yeah, I liked that."

He'd shared more secrets than she'd expected. "I'm sorry about your parents." She knew just how deep of a blow losing them must have been. "I... lost mine, too. When I was seventeen." *Just a month away from my eighteenth birthday.*

"What happened?"

It was better to tell him now, so he could hear her side, and not just read the cold facts on a computer screen later. "Sometimes, people can't let you go."

His eyes narrowed.

"I had a boyfriend back then. Smart, super smart guy. And intense. But he…he started planning out my life for me. *Our* life. Only it wasn't a life I wanted. I had my own plans. A different college that I wanted to attend. A whole different life that waited for me." She pulled in a slow breath that seemed to chill her lungs. "Benjamin didn't understand that. He thought someone else was pressuring me. That my parents were trying to pull us apart."

"Casey…"

"So one night, he broke into my house and he killed them."

She saw the shock flash on his face.

"I heard the gunshots and that was what woke me up. I ran downstairs and found them, and he was still standing over them. He *smiled* at me and lifted his hand up, telling me that it was time for us to go."

His eyes had widened. "What did you do?"

"My mother was still alive. I could see her breathing. I ran to her and I screamed for him to get away. I put my hands on her chest, trying to stop that blood from pumping out of her." She lifted her hand away from him. Sometimes, she could swear that she still saw blood on her. "He grabbed me, yanked me up. Told me we were leaving."

The room was so quiet.

"I wasn't going to leave them. I told him that… and he put the gun to my head."

His hands flew up and curled around her shoulders. *"Casey."*

That hadn't been her name, not back then. Back then, she'd been Cassidy.

Cassidy, I did this for you! All for you! We can have everything now! We can be together now!

"He said if I didn't leave with him, he was going to kill me."

Josh's fingers bit into her skin.

"I knew he meant those words, too. We'd been dating for six months, and I'd never seen him for what he really was, not until that terrible night. He was going to kill me. My mom couldn't even pull in a full breath. Her blood was everywhere. My dad was *gone*, and if I didn't walk out of that house with Benjamin, I was going to die, too." Her voice was brittle, as if she were on the verge of breaking. She wasn't, though. She hadn't broken back then…

I won't break now.

"The neighbors must have heard the gunshots. The police came swarming up just as we stepped outside. Benjamin fired at them and I ran…"

She could never forget that night.

"I felt the bullet hit me in the back. I slammed down into the ground. I tried to look back and I saw that Benjamin was getting ready to shoot at me again. He was aiming for me. He wasn't letting me go."

Bam! Bam! Bam!

"But the cops fired—they kept firing until they took him down. Benjamin died on my front porch."

Josh's face seemed carved from granite. A hard, stone mask, but his eyes blazed with emotion.

"I stayed in the hospital afterward. I was lucky— the bullet had missed my spine. Lucky… I was alive and everyone else was gone. I stayed in the hospital, and I hated that place. I *hated* what had become of my life." Just as she'd hated Benjamin. It was easy to hate the dead.

"No wonder you wanted out of the hospital."

Her lips twisted. "And that's the same reason I don't have any current lovers to give your FBI buddy. I don't trust easy. Relationships aren't really my thing."

"Victims are." His fingers stroked down her arms. "That's why you're a reporter, isn't it? You're doing the profiles on the victims in your stories."

"I try to make sure they get the justice they need." Because there had been no justice for her—her family had just been gone. "I changed my name because I wanted to put the past behind me. I'd always wanted to be a reporter, and I wasn't going to let him take that from me. But I didn't want everyone seeing *me* as the victim. I didn't want it to be about me. I didn't…" Her breath expelled on a sigh. "I didn't want to be the story."

But she was. Again.

His touch was so careful on her skin. "I had you all wrong."

She swallowed. "You mean…when you called me a vulture?"

"Did I apologize for that yet?" Josh winced. "Because I am sorry. And I think we need to start over. Way over."

But Casey shook her head. "I don't want to do that. You're the guy who came rushing to my rescue. I'm not forgetting that."

"Bull. You saved yourself."

"I won't be destroyed again." When you had nothing left, you learned to fight. She'd learned and she would never forget.

His hand slid under her chin. "I don't think anything can destroy you."

He had no clue. When she'd been in that hospital, everyone else gone, she'd felt utterly destroyed. The machines had beeped around her, the nurses had slipped in and out of her room, and she'd felt like a ghost. Everything had been surreal. And the days had just passed—the world had kept going—while she was alone in her bed.

His face was so close to hers. Their lips were close. She'd just bared her soul to him. But it was better that way, right? Better for her to tell him instead of him reading those dark details without her in some neat little file at the FBI. "It's your turn." Her voice had grown husky. "You have to tell me something…"

"I want you."

Her eyes widened. That was *not* what she'd expected.

"I think you're the most beautiful woman I've

ever seen, and I know I should be keeping my hands off you."

His hands weren't off. They were on.

"You need comfort right now. You need sympathy. You need care."

Maybe what I need...is you.

She'd had too much sympathy. Didn't he get that? She'd changed her name, changed everything so that she could be stronger. So people would stop looking at her with pity in their eyes.

"I'm not an easy guy, Casey."

No, she didn't think he was.

"I like danger. I take risks. Emotions haven't been a big part of my life. Usually, when I see something I want, I go after it."

And he wanted her.

But he wasn't moving. A few more inches, and his mouth would be on hers. He was staring at her with his intense gaze. She licked her lips. His stare heated even more. "Why...why aren't you kissing me?" Casey asked.

His pupils seemed to double in size as the darkness spread in his stare. His nostrils flared. "Because I'm trying to be different...with you. You deserve different."

He let her go. He stood up. Headed for the door.

That was it? He was...leaving?

"I don't want pity from you." She rose to her feet. Her hands fisted at her sides. "I told you my story because I knew you'd figure out the truth. But now you're acting like I'm different. You're acting like—"

"You matter." His back was to her. His words came out sounding rough. "So I'm trying not to mess this up. I didn't expect you." He looked back at her. "But I'm trying to do this *right*. You confessed your darkest pain to me, and I'm *not* going to pounce on you. I'm going to give you space. I'm going to give you whatever you need—"

Because he was a protector, straight to his core. Did he even get that? She'd asked why he'd been a SEAL, why he'd joined the FBI…and the truth was right there.

To protect.

She closed the distance between them and put her hand on his shoulder. "Neither one of us has exactly had an easy life." But no one was guaranteed easy. "Sometimes right doesn't matter. Sometimes there isn't a wrong." In that moment, there was only one thing she wanted. "Kiss me."

A muscle flexed along the hard line of his jaw. "Casey…"

"If I'm really what you want, then kiss—"

He pulled her into his arms. His mouth took hers. She'd expected some passion. Some excitement. What she didn't expect was the absolute explosion of feeling that she experienced when his mouth took hers.

The kiss rocked Casey straight to her core. Every cell in her body seemed to ignite. Her hands grabbed on to his arms, her nails sank into his shirt and she pulled him closer. He'd crushed her to his body, and his hard strength pressed against her. He kissed her with a hunger that she couldn't deny, with a need that called to her. Her lips parted even more for him, and his tongue thrust into her mouth. She moaned and her body rubbed against his. Her skin felt so sensitive, primed, and the way the man kissed…

His mouth pulled from hers. She immediately bit back a protest.

"I…shouldn't have done that."

No, he should have done a whole lot more.

"My job is to keep you safe." He stepped back and let her go.

She stared at him. Her heart was racing. Her breath came in quick pants.

His heated stare swept over her. "But I'm not apologizing."

Good. She hadn't asked for an apology.

"And it's probably going to happen again."

Probably? "Count on it," she said.

His lips kicked into a half smile. "But it will *not* happen until your twenty-four-hour concussion watch is over."

"Josh—"

He held up a hand, stopping her when she stepped toward him. "I don't think you understand how much I want you." His smile vanished. "And how fragile my control is where you're concerned."

She could still taste him.

"Stay in here and relax a while," he said. "I need to…talk a few things over with Tucker."

Translation—he needed to go and tell Tucker about her past. Some of that wonderful warmth she'd felt faded.

"Benjamin is dead," she said quietly. "He was an only child. His mother passed away last year, and his father—he died a few years ago. There is no one in his family who would be seeking any kind of crazed vengeance against me." Her shoulders straightened. "And there is no one that I've let get close since then."

"I guess that depends on your definition of close."

She wasn't sure she followed.

"For some guys, it's all about the fantasy. You don't realize you're starring in that fantasy until it's too late." He reached for the doorknob. "I'll be right outside if you need me, okay? I have to talk with Tucker and check in with the rest of the team." His gaze slid to the phone on the bed. "No more phone calls, okay? Not today."

Then he was gone. Maybe she should have felt like a prisoner, locked away but…she felt safe—for the moment, anyway.

HE'D MISREAD CASEY. Totally judged her wrong. He'd let his past interactions with reporters get to him, and Josh hadn't seen her for the woman she was.

His blinders were off. He saw her now. He always would.

He marched back into the den.

Tucker was tapping away at his laptop, but when he saw Josh, he put down the computer and raised his brows. "How'd that chat go?"

"Her past isn't pretty." Talk about an understatement. "But it might be a lead we can use." He headed toward Tucker. There were a few details about the recent murders that hadn't made it to the press. A deliberate move.

"She's linked, just like the other victims," he said, making sure to keep his voice low. "She was the victim of a violent crime, too."

Tucker's jaw hardened. "He definitely has a victim type, doesn't he?"

Yes, he did… The perp liked a survivor. The first victim, Kylie Shane, had been attacked when she was sixteen years old. She'd been stabbed twice, but had managed to get away from her attacker. During the exam of her body, the ME had found those old scars.

The second victim, Bridget Donaldson, had been the victim of a hit and run when she'd been just fifteen. She'd been walking home from school and the driver hadn't even slowed when he hit her. Bridget had spent four weeks in the hospital. But she'd survived.

Just as Kylie had survived.

And Tonya Myers? An arsonist had set her home on fire, while Tonya and her sister had been inside. The sister had died, but Tonya escaped. She'd suffered second-degree burns on her legs, but she'd *survived.*

As Casey had survived.

"Casey's high school boyfriend killed her family and tried to kill her." Rage boiled inside him, a hot blackness that wanted to consume Josh. "She even changed her name after the attack, tried to become someone new."

Tucker's gaze was considering. "But our perp found out her secrets."

Tell me all of your secrets.

Tucker tapped his hand on the side of the couch. "It's not just about the victims being attractive women in their twenties, not about them being outsiders. These women were survivors."

"Were," Josh pointed out darkly. Because that was the point to note. "They survived until he got hold of them." And then the killer had made sure that they didn't escape death. He'd made so sure…he'd given Kylie, Bridget and Tonya a watery grave.

No escape.

"Your Casey survived," Tucker noted.

She isn't mine. But he wished that she were.

Tucker's face became grim. "He isn't going to let her walk away. If he's choosing these women specifically because of their past, he isn't going to find an easy replacement for Casey. And her escaping him… he'll take it as a personal attack. She *survived* what he did to her. He can't let that happen."

"He'll come after her again." Even as he said it, Josh hated those words.

"Yes." Tucker wasn't the sugarcoating type. With

his life, Josh knew he couldn't be. Neither of them could be. "We have to be ready."

They would be. Because Josh was not going to let Casey be hurt. He'd stand between her and any threat that came.

Chapter Seven

The sun was shining. The waves were pounding against the shore—she could hear them through the open balcony door in her room. And Casey didn't feel so safe any longer.

She opened the bedroom door and marched down the hallway. She headed into the kitchen and spotted Josh's back as he leaned inside the open refrigerator.

"I can't do this. I can't just…stay here, indefinitely. It's been over twenty-four hours since you brought me here, and I'm already going crazy." Her words tumbled out too fast. *Twenty-four hours*. Twenty-four very slow hours had elapsed while she'd been in that penthouse. "I need to talk to Katrina again. I need to do *something* to help find that freak who attacked me. And just staying in here while that guy is out there, possibly lining up someone else in his sights—that isn't *me*."

The man rose and she saw his dark hair. Hair that didn't belong to Josh. Her mouth dropped open a bit. She'd been so sure—

Tucker Frost stared at her, one brow raised. "I told him we'd be lucky if you lasted a day." He shut the refrigerator door behind him.

She glanced around the quiet penthouse. "Where is Josh?"

"At the sheriff's station. He needed to talk with Hayden Black."

He'd left without telling her. Just…left? Why did that make her angry?

"He'll be back soon—don't worry."

"I'm not worried," she immediately replied. She wasn't. She— "The disposable phone vanished from my room."

"Right. Yes. Josh took it. With him leaving, he wanted to make sure you didn't get the urge to call your news buddies in his absence."

So Josh hadn't trusted her. "I can't keep staying here." Each word was snapped. *Take a breath, Casey. Calm down.* But she was going stir crazy. She hadn't been outside in a day and staying cooped up, with nothing to do…it just gave her time to think about her attack. Over and over again. "I want to help."

"You're the only witness, the only survivor. Trust me, you *are* helping."

"No, I'm hiding—there's a difference." And she'd come to a hard realization during the long hours that had passed. "If someone else dies while I'm here, that death will be on me."

"No," Tucker said flatly. "That will be on the killer out there. He's the one who takes the life—

he's the one who has the responsibility." His hand raked over his face. "No matter what anyone else will tell you."

"I came here yesterday because the doctor said that in order for me to be released from the hospital, I needed someone to watch me. Josh said he'd take that job. And I—I wasn't quite myself." She'd wanted a safe harbor. "But there has to be more than just…*this*. If I don't contact my boss again, I may not have a job. I can't just sit here, waiting forever."

The door opened behind her. She whirled around and saw Josh standing in the entranceway. His gaze slid from her to Tucker.

"Happened just like I said," Tucker murmured. "Barely a day and she wants out."

"What *she* wants," Casey stressed, "is to help. To be of use. Not to be hidden away." She hurriedly crossed the room and stood in front of Josh. "I want to help the investigation. I'll keep a guard with me— I'll play by the FBI's rules, but staying here indefinitely just can't happen."

He shut the door and secured the lock. "Your face is currently on every TV in the area. Your story is showing constantly."

She'd rather expected as much.

"You go out into the city, and you won't be helping. You'll be swarmed by your fellow reporters. They'll close in like sharks."

"But—"

"I need you."

She blinked. Those hadn't been the words she expected.

"Sheriff Black called me to his office today because there's been a...development."

A development?

"Before the attack, you'd been working to get an interview with Theodore Anderson."

"Yes." She nodded. "He hasn't spoken to any reporters, and I wanted to interview him. I know it was a long shot, and his lawyer kept denying my request but—"

"He's not denying it anymore. Theodore Anderson wants to talk. But only to you."

Her eyes widened. "You aren't serious."

"Dead serious. *That's* why I was talking to Sheriff Black. Anderson has been completely shut down since his trial, but suddenly, the guy is saying he'll speak freely...to you. He doesn't want his attorney present—he said he didn't give a damn about his rights. He just wants to see...you."

She tucked a lock of hair behind her ear. "My producer must be freaking out."

"Yeah, I met him. Dear *Tom* was camped out at the sheriff's station, demanding to see you. He wants to make certain you're all right, and he wants his star reporter going in for that interview."

She couldn't miss that opportunity. "Theodore Anderson could have killed other victims. He hasn't said a word to the cops—if he will really speak freely, there is so much I could learn from him."

Tucker had come up to stand at her side. "The FBI has been wanting him to talk…"

"Yeah." Josh rubbed the back of his neck. "And he's said jack to everyone so far. But this could be a chance…"

Excitement had her rising onto the balls of her feet. "You're going to let me out of here so I can see him?"

His hand fell. His eyes glittered. "*We're* going to see him."

"I don't—"

"You just agreed to keep a guard with you. I'm that guard. And I'll be going with you on the little visit with Anderson. Consider me your new assistant."

"But…" But she didn't know what to say.

"I don't trust Anderson," Tucker said quietly.

"Neither do I," Josh immediately agreed.

It was hard to trust a convicted murderer.

"And for him to want to see you, Casey, right after your attack…" Josh whistled. "I don't like it, not at all. Despite being locked up, he would still have access to the news in prison. He'll know what happened to you."

Her mind was spinning and there was a dark suspicion that she couldn't ignore. For Anderson to want to talk with her *now*, after she'd escaped that creep with the knife… "There's more here."

Tucker cleared his throat. "There's an...option we may need to explore."

Her head tilted toward him.

"Two serials of this nature, both hunting in Hope... perhaps they are connected."

Her lips parted. "You think the guy who took me *knows* Theodore Anderson?"

Tucker shrugged. *Not* an answer. "I think we can't overlook any possible connections. At this time, everyone has been operating under the idea that Anderson committed his crimes on his own."

"But what if he didn't?" she whispered.

"What if," Tucker continued, "there was always someone in the background?"

She understood exactly what Tucker and Josh wanted. "You need me to talk to Anderson and see if he'll reveal anything about this perp."

Josh didn't look happy, but he said, "It's too coincidental that he wants to see you now. We can't let this chance pass us by. We need to go in and see what the guy will reveal." But he seemed hesitant. "Are you up for this? Be sure..."

She'd interviewed killers before. She'd stared straight into eyes that she knew were pure evil. Casey's chin lifted. "I'm up for this."

"I'll be with you every step of the way," he promised.

THEODORE ANDERSON WAS being held in a maximum security facility. Getting in to see him took some time, and Josh made sure he stayed with Casey every moment. Once they finally cleared security, he led the way into the small conference room that they would use for their session. A table waited inside, and a video camera had already been set up for the talk. As part of the deal for that little one-on-one, the FBI would be getting the video footage. Later, once they'd reviewed it thoroughly, the Bureau would turn over the video to Casey and her producer, Tom Warren.

That was the deal.

He glanced toward the one-way mirror that lined the wall on the right. Tucker was behind that mirror, watching and getting ready to make his observations. Hayden Black was in there, too. Hayden had to be kept away from the prisoner. Things were too personal between them. Anderson had gone after the woman Black loved, a woman who happened to be an FBI agent herself.

And Hayden wasn't exactly the forgiving sort.

Don't blame him a bit.

"You know the questions to ask?" Josh asked as he paced the room. Anderson would be arriving any moment.

Casey shot him a slightly annoyed look. The bruising on her cheek had faded a bit today. He still hated the reminder of her pain. And he couldn't wait to find the jerk who'd hurt her.

"I'm a professional," she told him, a crisp edge to

her voice. "I really don't need my questions hand-fed to me."

No, she didn't. But those prepared questions had come straight from Tucker because the guy was trying to get into Anderson's head.

She pulled out a chair at the table. She sat, with her back perfectly straight, right before the door opened. A guard entered first—young, with dark brown hair and dark eyes.

The prisoner came in after him. The man was tall, fit and wore the garish orange of a prison jumpsuit. The lines on Theodore Anderson's face were deep, and his blond hair had thinned. His tan complexion had turned pallid since he'd been locked up. He shuffled forward, and Josh saw the shackles that connected from the lock around the prisoner's ankles to his bound wrists.

Another guard followed Theodore inside. The two guards kept their attention on Theodore, obviously worried he might lunge at the pretty reporter as they steered him toward the table. But he didn't lunge. Theodore just kept moving with those slow, shuffling steps.

A few moments later, he'd taken the seat across from Casey. His gaze swept over her, narrowing a bit when he saw the swelling and bruising on her cheek.

Josh rolled back his shoulders. He was standing to the side, his back against the wall as he stared at the prisoner—and at Casey. One wrong move from the prisoner, and the guards wouldn't have to attack because Josh would be on the guy.

"Mr. Anderson." Casey's voice was smooth, calm. "Just why did you agree to see me today?"

He was silent—a silence that stretched a bit too long. Tucker had coached a disgruntled Casey before she went into the prison—trying to tell her how to use interrogation techniques. Casey had been adamant that she already knew plenty of techniques to use. And as she'd told Tucker and Josh, it wasn't her first time interviewing a murderer. Not her first time, not even her fifth.

"Sorry about what he did to you," Theodore said, hitching his head forward. His eyes were bright in his pale face. "Such a shame…"

"He?" Casey prompted.

Theodore smiled. Josh didn't like that smile. Too cold. Too calculating. A monster's smile. But then, he was staring at a man who'd killed his own daughter. Was there a worse monster?

"I heard the guards talking about what happened to you." With his bound hands, Theodore gestured to the men beside him. "Seems the good people of Hope have more to fear than just me these days."

"The people of Hope feared you for a very long time. A killer living right among them—someone they never suspected." Her voice was still low and unemotional. "They felt sympathy for you, pity, because you lost your daughter." She gave a brief pause.

"They never realized that you were the one who'd murdered her."

Theodore's hands slammed down onto the table. *"That wasn't my fault!"*

Josh—and the guards—immediately surged forward, but Casey waved them back. "Then whose fault was it?"

"Christy was never supposed to die! You think I'd go after my own daughter? No, *no.* I had a victim. Jill…sweet little Jill, but she got away. She got away and she messed *everything* up for me."

Jill… Jillian West. The woman Hayden loved. The FBI agent who'd finally learned the truth about Theodore Anderson.

"Christy was the one good thing in my life." Theodore's shoulders slumped forward. "After she was gone…I was only left with…*him.*"

"Him?" Casey prompted.

Theodore looked up at her, squinting. "You ever stare straight at evil, Casey Quinn?"

She's staring at it right now. So was Josh. He knew evil when he saw it. But Casey didn't speak, she just waited.

The woman does know how to work an interrogation. She would have made a good FBI agent.

"I have. I saw it…in his eyes." Theodore licked his lower lip. "He's the one who took you. He's the one who hurt you. Who hurt the others… I tried to keep him in check all those years, but now that I'm locked up in here…there's nothing to stop him."

Every muscle in Josh's body locked down.

"You know the identity of the man who abducted me?" Casey asked, leaning forward.

Josh didn't like that. He didn't want her getting so much as another inch closer to Theodore Anderson.

The prisoner nodded. "He took you…and I heard what he did to those other women, too. He killed them. Always knew he'd be a killer."

"Who is he?" Casey's voice was strained now.

"Guess sometimes, it *is* in the blood, huh?" He expelled a long sigh, then looked regretful as he said, "The apple didn't fall so far away, now did it?"

And Josh knew what the guy was going to say, even before Theodore Anderson smiled.

"The man who took you," Theodore said, "the man who killed those others…it's my son, Kurt."

JOSH KEPT HIS body next to Casey's as they exited the interrogation room. After his big reveal, Theodore Anderson had locked down, refusing to say another word. Apparently, he'd wanted to point the finger at his son.

And he had.

Josh opened the door to the right and led Casey inside the observation room. Tucker was on the phone.

"Yeah, that's right," Tucker barked into the phone. "I want to know where Kurt Anderson is right now. Find the guy and bring him to the sheriff's station. I want to talk to him…Yes, yes, get him there, and

I'll meet you." He hung up and swung to face Casey. "Good job, Ms. Quinn—"

"Casey," she cut in. "Just…Casey, okay?" she slid away from Josh and moved toward the observation window. The glass showed them the now empty interrogation room. "Do we believe the guy? I've talked to Kurt Anderson a few times since coming to town."

Behind her back, Josh and Tucker shared a long look.

"Kurt struck me as someone who was fighting a lot of grief and anger. He'd just found out that his own father murdered his sister years ago…and that he'd *lived* with that killer. He was hurting, but for him to suddenly start killing…" One shoulder lifted in a weak shrug. "Does that fit?" She looked back at Tucker, then at Josh.

"It *could* fit," Tucker allowed. But he didn't say more.

Josh just watched Casey. He was worried she was pushing herself too hard.

Her full lips pressed together. "You are *not* shutting me out now."

"We should get going," Josh announced. "It's a drive back to—"

"*I* did this interview for you both. I got the guy to talk. Now you're trying to pull some FBI rank and not share with me?" Her cheeks flushed. "Not cool, gentlemen."

"You're a reporter," Tucker gently reminded her.

When her eyes turned to slits, Josh figured she didn't like—or need—that reminder. "And this is an active investigation. There's only so much we *can* say to you."

"I want the guy who attacked me caught! I want Kylie, Bridget and Tonya to have justice! I'm *helping* here. What happened to us being a team? What happened to that?" Her gaze raked them. "Or are we only a team when the two of you want to use me?"

"You're the one who insisted on doing this," Tucker replied, voice quiet. "And you're the one who'll get to air the footage later. You'll have the scoop of the century, won't you? So I think it's a win for you."

Her expression hardened.

No, it wasn't a win. Tucker was misjudging her, the same way Josh had. Josh crossed to her side. "We should get going."

Her gaze jumped to his face. "Do you think it's Kurt?"

He thought it was possible, but his stare slid to Tucker and he replied, very carefully, "Just because a killer's in the family, it doesn't mean you have bad blood. Each person makes his or her own choices."

"I'm going to find Kurt," Tucker stated. "Josh, we'll talk later." Then he turned on his heel and marched out.

"It's hitting too close to home for him," she murmured. "Isn't it?"

Yes, the case was. Because Tucker had a killer in

the family, too. One who'd come far too close to destroying everything that Tucker loved.

Josh caught Casey's hand in his. His fingers slid over her wrist, and he felt the quick jump of her pulse. "Let's get out of here."

"You still didn't tell me whether or not you think the killer could be Kurt Anderson."

No, he hadn't told her, not yet. "Just how many times did you talk to Kurt?"

"Three times." They walked down the narrow corridor, past the guards. The security doors were opened for them, one after the other. Soon they had cleared the checkpoints. Josh took his gun back and adjusted his holster.

"The last time I saw him…" She'd been quiet as they passed the guards. "We had a brief dinner on Friday night."

She'd gone to dinner with the guy? Dinner…the night before she'd been abducted.

"I wanted to hear his side of things." They walked out of the facility. The sun was bright, beating down on them. "He lost his sister. He was just as much of a victim as—"

"Casey!" a man's voice boomed.

Josh tensed and his body immediately moved in front of Casey's. His hand went to his weapon.

A man with black hair and thin-framed glasses rushed forward. He wore a suit and had a flashy watch around his wrist. A short-haired woman was behind him—Josh recognized Katrina, Casey's camerawoman. And, unfortunately, he recognized the man, too. Tom Warren. Casey's producer.

"Knew you'd get the exclusive!" Tom cried out. He tried to reach out and touch Casey. Josh just moved his body and prevented that touch. "Wait— what the hell are you doing?"

Protecting Casey.

Tom's gaze sharpened on him. "Look, Agent Duvane, I get that you saved Casey, and I'm grateful, but you can relax. I'm not any threat to her."

Josh didn't relax.

A trickle of sweat slid down Tom's temple. "Hey... I've got an idea." He flashed a smile. "It would be great if we could get you both on camera. You know, some footage of Casey and the agent who saved her." He motioned to Katrina. "Get the gear from the van."

"Not happening," Josh said flatly. "And for the record, Casey saved herself."

"Right, right, yes, but I haven't gotten all of those *details* yet." Tom's smile slipped. "Because I kept being told that I can't speak to my own employee."

Josh didn't want the guy talking to Casey. And the other woman, Katrina, was shifting nervously from foot to foot. Obviously, she was wondering if she should follow Tom's orders and rush to get the camera or if she should stay put.

"Casey." Tom's voice deepened. It took on a personal, almost possessive edge as he said her name. "I've been worried about you."

Katrina slanted a quick, hard stare toward her boss.

Casey slid closer to Josh's side. "I'm okay."

"Your face." His eyes were absolutely horrified as he stared at her cheek. "Katrina, get the camera." He stepped toward Casey, lifting his hand to touch her cheek. "People need to see—"

Josh caught the guy's wrist before Tom could touch Casey. "See what? Her pain?"

Tom's pale blue eyes narrowed. "They need to see the damage that the monster did to her. When people see real pain, up close and personal, they have a more visceral reaction. The public loves Casey. They relate to her. We show the world what that SOB did to her, and everyone will be hunting for him."

"Everyone is hunting for him now," Casey said and her shoulder brushed against Josh's arm. "But it's hard to find a killer when no one knows what he looks like."

Josh let go of Tom's hand.

"You didn't get a look at his face?" Now Tom sounded disappointed.

She shook her head.

"You must have noted *something* about him. Something distinct that we can lead with. His voice. Mannerisms. A stutter—"

"You aren't leading with anything," Josh said flatly. "Casey is leaving with me, right now."

Tom's mouth opened, closed and then opened again. Finally, he sputtered, "She works for me!"

Josh really didn't like the producer. "And she's in *my* protective custody. For the moment, I need her to stay off the radar. By going on-air again, she might just make the killer focus even more on her."

Casey sighed. "He's already come for me once. I don't know that there can be *more* of a focus."

Josh turned toward her. "Going on camera would be like shining a spotlight on yourself right now." He didn't want that danger gathering around her again. "Give me a little more time." Time for them to find Kurt. To bring him in for questioning. Time to analyze the situation more. "Just— I'm not asking for forever. I'm just asking for you to stay off the air a little longer, let the agents and Sheriff Black do their jobs. Give us a little more time."

"You can't hold Casey prisoner," Tom huffed. "You can't keep her trapped in protective custody. I'm her boss, but I'm her friend, too. And I'm not going to let you trample over her rights!"

He wasn't trampling over anything. He was trying to keep her alive.

"We're both her friends," Katrina muttered, her lips curving down.

Tom nodded. "Kat and I will stay with Casey. We'll make sure she's safe." He waved toward Casey, as if expecting her to just walk toward him. "You really think I'd leave my top reporter without a guard under these circumstances? One phone call, and I'll have *two* bodyguards at her side at all times. I mean, I appreciate your efforts, Agent Duvane, but isn't your focus more on diving into the water? Evidence retrieval? Perhaps you're just not suited to this role at all."

He would so enjoy driving his fist into that guy's face. But an FBI agent wasn't supposed to do stuff like that. He wasn't supposed to *want* to hurt a civilian. "My focus right now is on Casey. Her safety is the priority for me."

Tom's lips thinned. "Casey? Come on, you know I can get you the best protection money can buy. I can get—"

She slowly exhaled. "Thank you, Tom, but I'm going with the FBI right now. They've promised me an exclusive regarding new developments in this case, and the closer I stay to Agent Duvane, the better chance I have of being on scene when the killer is apprehended."

A gleam lit Tom's eyes. "They're that close to catching him?"

No, they weren't. And he didn't remember making the promise Casey was talking about.

"I'm going to stay with Agent Duvane for at least the next twenty-four hours," Casey continued, her voice brisk, as if she'd reached a decision and that was all there was to it. "Then I'll be ready to go on-air again."

Twenty-four hours. Well, that was better than nothing.

But Tom shook his head. "I need a report *sooner* than that. You have people waiting for you—you have—"

"Twenty-four hours," Josh said flatly. "You heard the lady." And if he had twenty-four more hours without that Tom jerk breathing down their necks, that would sure be a sweet deal to him.

"Everyone will tune in for the story, Tom," Casey promised. "You know they will."

And he could tell by Tom's expression that, yeah, the guy knew she was telling the truth.

"I'm hoping you got something good in that place," Tom said as he dragged his hand across his jaw. "Theodore freaking Anderson—can't believe he finally agreed to an interview with you. I've been after that guy for ages. Casey, you are the queen."

"We're leaving." Josh didn't like standing out in the open with Casey, not even in a scene where dozens of guards were patrolling the grounds. He wanted her away from there—or maybe, maybe he just wanted her away from Tom.

"Here, take this." Tom pulled a phone from his pocket and pushed it into Casey's hand. "I think the cops took yours from the hotel, and I wanted to make sure you could contact me, whenever you needed me." He slanted a hard stare toward Josh. "I got the feeling the last call was made on someone else's phone, and I wanted you to have the freedom to call me anytime."

The guy just seriously didn't understand what protective custody actually meant.

Then Tom pulled Casey in for a hard, tight hug. "I was worried." His voice had turned gruff. "You scared me. You're too important to the show—to me. Nothing can happen to you."

Josh saw Katrina's face harden. She quickly glanced away from Casey and Tom.

"Agent Duvane will make sure I stay safe." Casey eased from Tom's hold. "And thanks for the phone." She slid it into her pocket. Then she reached for Josh's hand. "Ready?"

Hell, yes. He curled his fingers around hers and stalked toward the waiting SUV. He opened her door, made sure she was in securely, then he slammed the door shut. He glanced back and saw that Tom was still watching them.

Or maybe the guy is just watching her. Tom certainly seemed to have a personal interest in Casey. Josh headed around the vehicle and yanked his door shut after he'd jumped inside. He cranked the engine. Tom was still watching. "Your boss wants you."

Her laugh was startled. "What? No, I told you already…he's involved with Katrina. One of those friends-with-benefits type deals."

Not really friends if the guy was her boss.

"He wants you," Josh said flatly. He'd read the guy's expression too clearly.

"Well, I'm not into him. Sleeping my way to the top has never been on my agenda. And I can't do the with-benefits routine because—" But she broke off, not saying more.

He drove them out of there. "Because of your past."

"Trust is hard. Being that intimate with someone… I don't like to take risks."

No, he got that. But what he didn't get… "Why didn't you go with them?" Tom had given her an out right then and there, but Casey hadn't taken it.

"Because I wanted to stay with you."

"I didn't promise you an exclusive." The Bureau brass would freak if they thought he'd been making any side deal with her. "The only thing on the table was your access to the footage from that little sit-down with Anderson." A sit-down that had not gone the way he expected.

Kurt Anderson. He'd met the guy before, too. The man had seemed shaken, grief-stricken. And he'd been filled with a lot of rage. But Josh had thought all of that rage was directed at Kurt's father.

Had he been wrong?

"I know, Josh." Her soft sigh filled the car. "I lied," Casey admitted without even a hint of guilt.

He cast a quick glance toward her.

"I wanted to stay with you," Casey said again. "I…feel safe with you, okay? I mean, I've already told you the deepest, darkest secret that I have. You pretty much know me better right now than anyone else has known me in years."

Why did that make him feel good?

"Even though you didn't do an even secret exchange," she added.

Maybe he'd make that up to her.

"Tom can hire bodyguards, I know that. *I* can hire my own guards. But right now, I'm where I want to be." She paused. "But I do want a favor."

A favor?

"In return for agreeing to stay in federal custody a bit longer, in return for the solid I did you by interviewing Anderson, I want you to take me back to the scene of the crime."

He braked hard at the red light. *"What?"*

"I need to go back," she said. "I think if I go back, I might remember something. It's a technique I've had psychologists use with victims on my show before. I want to try. I want to go back to my hotel room, and then I want you to take me back to the beach house."

Someone honked behind him. He didn't move. "You know you can only get access to those locations if you're with me...or with another federal agent." Was that the real reason why she'd agreed to stay with him? "You realized that all along, though, didn't you?"

She gave a disappointed sigh. "Do you always see the bad in people first? Or do you—sometimes—stop to see any good?"

There wasn't always a lot of good in the world. The car behind him honked again, and Josh slowly accelerated.

"Come on, you know it's in your best interest for me to remember more, too. So why not just take me to the scene? I'll still be in protective custody. Your custody. And maybe I'll see something that jars my memory. Maybe I'll be able to find some

W e'd like to send you two free books like the one you are enjoying now. Your two books have a combined cover price of over $10 retail, but they are yours to keep absolutely FREE! We'll even send you 2 wonderful surprise gifts. You can't lose!

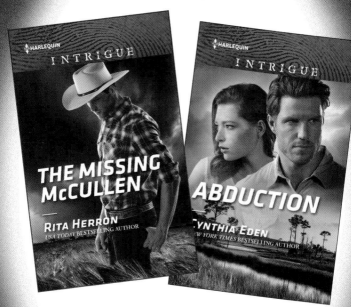

REMEMBER: Your Free Merchandise, consisting of **2 Free Books** and **2 Free Gifts**, is worth over $20 retail! No purchase is necessary, so please send for your Free Merchandise today.

Get TWO FREE GIFTS!
We'll also send you 2 wonderful FREE GIFTS (worth about $10 retail), in addition to your 2 Free books!

Visit us at:
www.ReaderService.com

Books received may not be as shown.

and pulled out his phone. His finger swiped across the screen and a slow smile stretched across his face. "Got you."

Unease coiled through her. Just who did the guy have?

"Come on. Get in the car." Now his words were clipped. "I'll drop you off in town and then take care of business." Impatience gritted beneath each word.

"You don't want me to get some scene shots of this place? For the show later?"

He huffed out a breath. "Yeah, yeah, just hurry, okay?"

She took out her equipment from the backseat. She turned away so that she could eye the buildings and the guards—

"Do you think they're sleeping together?"

Katrina almost dropped her bag. "What?"

"Casey and the agent. I noticed the way he touched her—and the way she touched him. Casey doesn't touch anyone, not as a rule."

No, she didn't. Katrina was just surprised that Tom had noticed that. Casey was always very careful with everyone. She kept them all at the same distance.

"She just met him," Katrina replied, trying to choose the right words. "Casey never gets involved with anyone that way—not right after they meet." Not the other woman's style. But then—Casey's style wasn't for attachments. She lived for her work. The woman was dedicated, tireless, and Katrina actually admired the hell out of her. Casey didn't take crap from anyone.

Good for her.

"You're right." He gave her an absent smile. "Still, it would have made for a good angle, right? The victim falling for the FBI agent."

She stiffened. "Casey's more than just a victim."

"Not right now, she isn't." He waved a hand toward her bag. "Get the shots. I don't have long." He looked back down at his phone. "I can't let her go."

That whisper of unease blew through her again as she turned back to the prison. So many guards—and such big, thick walls. *No escape.* And the idea of being locked away in a place like that...it chilled Katrina's blood.

Chapter Eight

Josh shut the hotel room door with a soft click. He looked around the darkened room, his body tense. Getting Casey into her old room had been easy enough. He'd just flashed his badge and gotten a personal escort up from the manager on duty. A manager who'd spent the whole elevator ride apologizing to Casey.

The security cameras at the hotel had *mysteriously* gone down the night she'd been taken. A glitch, or so the manager said. Josh wasn't ready to buy that line. Knowing the killer they were after, the way the guy left nothing to chance, Josh figured the perp had made sure the security feed wasn't working. The guy's bit of sabotage had protected him.

"Walk me back through the night," Josh instructed. Casey was standing in front of the balcony door. She looked hesitant, so uncertain. Not at all the way he was coming to view her.

Casey looked over her shoulder at him. "I was on the balcony, getting some air—"

"How long were you out there?" Josh asked.

"Just a few minutes. I was—I was thinking about everything that had happened that day."

Her voice had stumbled, just a bit. "Now who's lying?"

"Fine." She rolled back her shoulders. "I was out there, thinking about you, okay?"

His brows climbed. "Okay." She'd surprised him, again.

"I could hear the waves crashing, but I didn't hear anything from the hotel room. So when I turned around and the light was off, I had no idea that anyone was in here." She walked toward the phone that waited on the bedside table. "I was going to call the front desk, but he caught me from behind."

His gaze scanned the room. There weren't a whole lot of places for someone to hide in there, but if the room had been in total darkness, the perp would have just needed to find a corner, to stay still, to wait for her to come back... He walked toward her. The thick carpet swallowed his footsteps. "You turned on the lights before you left. *No one* was here?"

She turned to face him. "I didn't see anyone. Didn't hear anyone."

He stopped right in front of her. He *hated* that she'd been hurt. To think of that creep slamming her head into the wall, carrying her out of there... "I noticed the emergency exit is just one door down from your room. It would have been easy for him to take you out that way—no one would see you. The stairs there lead straight down to the parking lot below."

She swallowed. "And it's not like I was able to call out for help. I mean, Katrina was in the adjoining room—" Casey motioned to the door that connected the two rooms. "But I never even had a chance to scream for her."

He looked back at that door. He'd already known that Katrina had been in the room beside hers. The sheriff had interviewed the camerawoman—she hadn't been in her room that night. "It wouldn't have mattered if you *had* screamed for her," he said. "Katrina wasn't there."

"She— Oh. Right. Staying with Tom?"

"No. She said she was at a club down the road. Just dancing. I don't think she even realized you were gone until the next day." At least, that was what Katrina had told Hayden.

Casey tucked her hair behind her ear.

"But if Katrina wasn't here," Josh continued as he tilted his head. "Then maybe the perp used her room. Maybe he was in there, waiting for you to get back. He could have come straight in through the connecting door." He headed for that door now, wanting to test the lock. It was still secure but…if the guy had been on the other side, it would have been easy enough to gain entrance to Casey's room. And a perp who knew what he was doing? He wouldn't have left so much as a scratch on any of the doors.

"Is that what the FBI thinks happened? I mean,

I'm sure you've gotten together with your team and talked about it." There was an edge to her voice that had him glancing back. "Why don't *you* walk me through things and show me what happened. You be the perp. Show me what he did. Help me to re-create it all."

He locked his jaw. Yeah, the FBI had theories—and that was one of them. But for him to re-create things with her… *I don't want to scare Casey.* "Are you certain about that?"

She nodded once. "It's getting late. The sun is setting. It's dark enough in here that…it will be the same."

"It *won't* be the same." She needed to understand that. "You're safe with me. Nothing is going to happen to you."

"So…you *do* think he was in Katrina's room? That's what the FBI is going with?"

Treading carefully he said, "We believe the perp had been watching you for a few days. The night he attacked you, the guy knew that your camerawoman hadn't come back here. So, yes, we think it's possible that he was able to come inside, and he just waited… he could have even been out on the balcony next door, listening to see what you were doing while you stared down at the ocean. He could have been right there. Making sure you were alone."

"Then I guess you should have come up with me." Her words were said flippantly, and her tone was too brittle. "Then I wouldn't have been alone."

She turned away from him, but Josh grabbed her wrist. "I sure as hell wish I'd come up with you."

"I—I didn't mean that. You know, I—"

"I wish I'd been here. I wish I'd stopped the bastard."

She looked down at his hand as it gripped her wrist. Her wrist felt so small and fragile in his grasp. He wanted to pull her closer. Wanted to take her mouth beneath his once again. Would the need explode like wildfire in his veins when he kissed her once more? Had it been a fluke before?

Would it be even better this time?

The job. The case. Don't do this. Don't cross that line. He let her go. "You want to re-create the scene, then we'll recreate it." He motioned toward the balcony. "Go out and come back inside. I'll turn out the lights and we'll see if anything jars your memory." He paused. "If you're *sure*."

"I'm sure." But she licked her lips, a quick giveaway of her nerves. "Will you…will you come up behind me like he did?"

"Is that what you want?"

"I want to learn something new. I want to remember *something* else that can help us." She squared her shoulders. "Come up behind me. Grab me, just like he did. But, ah, don't do anything else, okay?"

"I won't." He kept his voice gentle for her. "If you get scared, just say stop and I will."

Casey gave a jerky nod. "Right. Got it." With

brisk steps, she headed for the balcony. She opened the door and stepped outside.

Josh turned off the lights.

THEY'D LOCATED KURT ANDERSON.

Tucker Frost jumped onto the coast guard vessel with Hayden Black. As soon as Theodore Anderson had identified his son as a suspect, Tucker had been on the phone and getting an APB out on the guy. Then Tucker had gotten lucky. A deputy at the marina remembered seeing Kurt head out on a boat.

"I talked to the guy who owns the boat rental company," Hayden said as the vessel shot away from the dock. "Apparently, Kurt has been taking out a rental a few days each week...and heading out into the Gulf of Mexico. Every time, he goes out alone."

Interesting, especially considering that the Sandy Shore Killer had a habit of heading into the Gulf, too...and dumping bodies. "He's sure Kurt goes out alone?"

"Yeah, Chaz—that's the guy's name, Chaz Fontel— Chaz said that Kurt told him that he needed time away."

Time away—or time to get rid of his victims?

The boat flew across the water. "Kurt almost killed his father." Hayden's voice was pitched to carry over the roar of the waves and the engine. "You probably read that in the files but..."

Tucker had. "But there are some details that don't

make it into the files," Tucker finished. He knew that truth firsthand.

"I saw the grief in his eyes. He was broken. Kurt loved his little sister, and to find out that his own father killed her—that shattered something in him." Hayden stared out at the water. "He was filled with anger and pain, but the grief was stronger than anything else. Jill and I—we stopped him before he could kill Theodore. We convinced Kurt that he wasn't like his old man. He wasn't a killer."

"He may not be," Tucker said. Blood didn't always tell. He was living proof of that. Or at least, he hoped he was. "We're just going by his father's words. Just following up with some questions. We don't have any evidence that directly ties him to the crimes." Not yet, they didn't.

Hayden's laugh was bitter. "We don't marshal a hunt like this just to ask a guy some questions. You and I are both thinking the same thing—he fits."

Kurt Anderson did match the profile that Tucker had been working up. He'd been building that profile slowly, not wanting to make any mistakes. Once upon a time, he'd been dead set on getting into the minds of killers. *Into proving that I wasn't one of them.* But then he'd backed off... Tucker had gotten more involved in the Violent Crimes Section at the Bureau. He'd worked Violent Crimes for a few years, but, recently, things had changed for him.

A new opportunity had developed at the Bureau,

one that had come courtesy of the best damn behavioral analysis specialist he'd ever met… Samantha Dark.

This case, the Sandy Shore Killer, was Tucker's
chance to prove that he could get back into the work.
His chance to prove that he could belong on the elite
team that Samantha Dark was leading.

He wouldn't screw up. And he *would* investigate
every viable suspect. Right then, Kurt Anderson appeared very, very viable.

"Why would he want to go out at night?" Tucker
mused. The sun had sunk beneath the sky. "Seems
to me that a person only does that if he has something to hide."

"I hope to God he isn't dumping a body." Hayden
exhaled then he glanced over at the man steering the
vessel. "Can you go faster?"

They were already going awfully fast.

"Kurt might not realize that the Chaz has a GPS
tracking device on every boat that he rents out. The
guy wasn't about to risk someone stealing his ves-
sels."

Tucker considered that. "Does Kurt always take
the same boat out?"

"Always, according to Chaz. Kurt requests the
exact same one."

"Then when we get him, we can check his log—
we can check his GPS and see exactly where he's
been going each time."

And if the guy had been going to the same locations where the bodies had been found… *We've got you.*

CASEY COULD HEAR the crash of the waves. She could smell the salty breeze. And she could feel her knees shaking. It was ridiculous to be so afraid but…

She was.

It's Josh. He won't hurt me. It's just Josh.

She opened the balcony door. Darkness waited inside. Josh had turned out the lights. Just like the perp had done. She took a step forward and hesitated.

It's Josh.

She should go toward the bedside table. That was what she'd done before. She'd gone to the table and reached for the phone. Casey tiptoed inside. But then she stilled. Where was Josh? She glanced around, but it was so dark. The light from the balcony just spilled inside a small bit, pooling near the sliding glass door. It was darkest in the room near the door that led to the hallway and…near the connecting door. The shadows were actually *the* thickest there. "Josh?" His name slipped from her.

"I'm here."

Her heart drummed too fast. His voice had come from those thick shadows near the connecting door.

She moved toward the phone. She reached for it—

His arms closed around her, holding her tightly. Fear stole her breath even as she opened her mouth to scream.

"It's okay." His whisper filled her ear. "I've got you." His lips brushed lightly against the shell of her ear. His scent hit her—the rich, masculine scent that seemed to surround him. It wasn't the bitter odor of oil that had tinted the air before and—

"I remember!" She spun in his arms. Grabbed his shoulders. "I remember...he smelled like oil! It was a bitter scent, and I caught it right before he... he shoved my head into that wall."

Darkness still surrounded them.

"You're sure it was oil?" Josh pressed.

"Absolutely! My dad—he used to have an old '66 Chevy that he restored on the weekends. I helped him, and nearly every Saturday we'd come back into the house with our hands stained with oil. I know that smell. I *remember* it." Joy filled her. It had worked. She'd remembered something new. Maybe something else would come to her. She was so excited that she pulled Josh toward her. She rose onto her toes, and her mouth pressed to his.

His body tensed. She felt his muscles go rock hard beneath her hands, and Casey started to pull away. She—

His hands locked around her, holding her tightly against him. His mouth opened, and his tongue thrust past her lips. He kissed her with a ferocious, consuming need. Kissed her with a dark desperation.

Kissed her the way only he could.

Desire burned through her blood. She'd known

only fear moments before, but the touch of his mouth against hers had ignited a firestorm inside her.

She wanted him.

And she was going to have him.

She'd spent years playing it safe in life—and what had that gotten her, exactly? She'd attracted the attention of another killer. She'd been targeted again. Maybe there was no safety. Maybe there was just the moment—the present. Maybe she should grab on tight to what she wanted and not let go.

She wanted him.

A moan built in her throat. His hands had slid down her back, and now they rested right over the curve of her hips. She wanted him to touch her, skin to skin. The barriers should be out of the way. They should both just let go.

And never look back.

But—

Josh slowly lifted his lips from hers. She heard the rasp of his breath and then he took a step away from her. Immediately, she missed his touch.

"You're playing a dangerous game," he said.

She touched her lips. Then her hand fell back to her side. "It's no game." She wasn't going to lie or pretend or be coy. Why waste time? "I want you, Josh."

"Casey..."

"You know I have trouble trusting the men in my life. But there is something about *you*." She didn't want to say that she was falling for him. It was too fast, too soon, but...

He's getting to me. I know it.

Casey swallowed. "I'm not playing games. We don't have time for games, and I don't like them, anyway. I want you. And you want me."

The darkness was around them, but all of her fear was gone.

"The question is," Casey continued quietly, "what do we do about that desire?"

THE SPOTLIGHT HIT the other boat. They'd found him. Tucker tensed.

"Kurt Anderson!" Hayden called out. "We need you to step forward so that we can see you—and put your hands up!"

Up…just in case the guy had a weapon. Up…just in case they were confronting an armed, desperate man.

It took a moment, but Kurt Anderson appeared. His hair was disheveled, his face covered by the thick growth of a beard, and in his right hand he held a beer can. His tall body wobbled a bit as he stood on the boat.

"What the hell? Hayden?" Kurt squinted against the bright light. "What's happening? Why are you out here?"

Tucker knew that Kurt and Hayden had once gone to school together. They'd been friends, a lifetime ago. Murder could change so much about a person.

"We're out here because we need to talk to you." Hayden's voice carried easily. "Is anyone else on your vessel?"

"No…" But Kurt looked back, at the cabin entrance behind him. "Just me."

Was the guy lying? "Mind if we take a look?" Tucker asked him. Even if the guy did mind, they'd be getting on that boat.

"Why would I care?" Kurt started to lower his hands.

"Keep them up, buddy," Tucker ordered. The guy could have a knife hidden on him. A gun. Any weapon that he could pull in a moment's notice, and Tucker wasn't in the mood for an attack.

He and Hayden boarded the other vessel. As they approached Kurt—

"What the hell?" Hayden demanded. "How many beers have you had?"

The scent of alcohol clung to the man, and Tucker had to kick a rolling beer can out of his way. He glanced around and counted at least seven empty beer cars on the deck.

"Just a few," Kurt said. His voice was slurred. "Makes it…easier, you know? Easier to forget…"

Hayden gave the man a pat down, then nodded toward Tucker. "He's clean."

"Damn right!" Kurt laughed. "Clean… Clean and my old man is dirty. A dirty killer. He killed and killed, and I just let it happen. Let it…happen…" He stumbled a bit.

Hayden righted the guy.

Tucker slipped below deck. He searched the boat and he saw…blood. A bloody shirt was tossed on the back of the small couch below deck. He didn't want to touch the shirt. There was no way he wanted to be responsible for contaminating evidence. Right next to that shirt, he saw a knife with a long, flat blade. Blood had dried on the tip of the blade. Pulling his gun, he headed back up the small flight of stairs.

"Where did that blood come from?" Tucker asked Kurt.

Kurt swung his head toward him. "Do I know you?" The fellow squinted at Tucker. The spotlight from the coast guard vessel still illuminated the scene.

"I'm Special Agent Tucker Frost." He stared at the suspect. "And, again, I'm asking you…where did the blood come from?"

Kurt didn't answer.

"There's a bloody shirt below deck," Tucker explained to Hayden.

And Casey stabbed her attacker.

"What happened?" Hayden demanded, his voice sharp.

"I was cutting some tangled fishing line and the knife slipped. I cut myself. No big deal." The last words came out together—fast, stumbling. Drunk. *Nobigdeal.*

It was a big deal. A very big deal.

"You know boating under the influence is against the law, don't you, Kurt?" Hayden's voice was hard.

"Not drunk. Just had…six. No, seven beers. Got to forget. Got to forget Christy. Makes it so much easier…"

"No, it just seems easier," Tucker responded. "When the haze of booze clears away, it will be even harder." He knew Hayden was going to arrest Kurt—the guy had given them the perfect reason to take him into the station. Once Kurt sobered up, they'd question him. They'd search the boat. They'd tear into his life.

And if he was guilty, he would pay.

He paced around the boat, heading back toward the motor. His nostrils flared. "You got yourself a leak, Kurt." The stench of oil was strong.

"That's why I stopped out here," Kurt muttered. "Boat's been giving me trouble. Every time I take it out… I told Chaz at the shop. Still not fixed…"

He gave the man a small smile. "I find myself very curious about your trips. Want to tell me…just where have you been going?"

Kurt blinked, and for the first time since they'd boarded his boat, worry flashed on his face. "What's going on? Why—why'd you come all the way out here after me? I haven't even had the chance to call in my Mayday yet."

No, he hadn't.

"We came looking for you," Tucker said, watching him closely. "Because your father sent us to find you…"

Chapter Nine

He should keep his hands off her. Josh *knew* that he should keep his distance from Casey. So why was he so desperate to get closer to her?

He secured the penthouse door behind them. The alarms were set. The cameras rolling. They were safe for the night.

"I wish we'd gone to the beach house." She stood a few feet away, gazing out at the darkness below her.

He shook his head, even though Casey couldn't see the movement. "Too dark. You wouldn't be able to see anything out there. You really want to re-create the scene, then we'll do it first thing tomorrow. We'll go back at dawn."

She looked back at him, a sad smile on her full lips. "Because that's when you found me."

A scene he'd never forget.

"You should go get some rest. I know it's been a long day for you." He glanced down at his phone. On their way to the penthouse, he'd tried calling Tucker, wanting to tell him about the oil scent, but he'd just gotten the guy's voice mail.

"Today wasn't as bad as yesterday. I didn't get attacked in my hotel room tonight. I consider that a win." She paused. "But I did get rejected."

His head snapped up.

That faint smile was still on her lips—a smile that didn't reach her dark, gorgeous eyes. "I get it," Casey added. "I'm not your type. I misread the situation. It won't happen again. I apologize if I...made you uncomfortable." She turned, obviously heading for the hallway—and her room. "I'll see you in the morning, okay?"

He should let her go. He should keep his mouth shut. He should— "You're not the only one with trust issues."

Casey stilled.

"You wanted to know my secrets? You wanted that fair exchange. Fine. Here goes." Josh released a long breath. "I trusted the wrong person, too. With fatal consequences."

Slowly, she turned back to face him. "Josh?"

"He was a man on my SEAL team. I thought he had my back. I thought he was a friend. In an instant, he turned on me—on us all. I lost two good men that day. And every day since, I've asked myself why I didn't see the truth about him sooner."

Her lips parted. "I've asked myself...why I didn't see the truth about Benjamin."

He understood her, and he knew—Casey understood him, too.

"I'm sorry," she whispered.

He didn't want her pity but—when he looked into her eyes, he realized she wasn't staring at him with pity. Just a kind of shared pain.

He'd never really thought about a future with anyone, but when he looked at Casey, he found himself imagining all kinds of things that he *shouldn't* be thinking. "My job is to keep you safe."

"I can hire a bodyguard for that. Tom was right on that point."

He was better than any bodyguard out there. "I'm an FBI agent," he tried again. "And you're—" But he broke off because he was staring into her eyes and he couldn't look away. He didn't want to look away. Her gaze was so deep and rich, and her lips were red and full. He loved her mouth. Josh was pretty sure her mouth was the sexiest thing he'd ever seen. That lower lip of hers was plumper than the top, and he kept having the urge to bite it.

He wanted his mouth all over her. He wanted to make sure that fear was the last emotion he would see in her gaze.

He. Wanted. Her.

So why was he fighting himself?

"I'm what, Josh?"

"You're the woman I want too much." She'd been honest with him. He'd give her the same in turn.

He heard her take a quick draw of breath. "How

can you want someone too much?" Casey took a step toward him. Then another.

If she kept coming to him, if she got close enough to touch…

He'd touch. He'd take. He wouldn't stop.

"I don't think once would be enough for me." He was trying to warn her. There was just something about Casey. From the moment he'd met her, Josh had been on high alert. Every muscle in his body had tensed. His focus had sharpened on her. "You're looking to escape aren't you? To get away from the darkness for a moment, but being with me won't take you away from the darkness." Too much darkness surrounded him. "I'm not the safe lover you want."

Another step. Her scent reached him. Sweet. Sexy. Casey. "You're an FBI agent. I think that probably makes you the safest lover I've ever had."

Carrying the badge, working on the right side of the law…she didn't get it. There were different kinds of safety. "I'd never hurt you." And he knew, even as he spoke, that he was setting out the terms. Because it *was* going to happen. They were going to happen. "I'd never hurt you physically, you have my word on that. I'd put myself between you and a threat any day of the week." He meant that. When he was with Casey, no threat would touch her. He'd make sure of it. And because of her past, he had to say, "You would never need to fear me."

She took another step. If he lifted his hands, he'd be able to touch her. But he didn't lift them, not yet. They needed to be very, very clear before they crossed this line. "There won't be any going back. No pretending in the morning that this didn't happen. Once won't be enough…" It was what he'd said before because he already knew he would want more. He wasn't sure he'd ever get enough of her. "I'm not an easy lover. But I'll give you so much pleasure you can't stand it."

Her eyes gleamed. "Promises, promises…"

"Yes." That was all he said.

She caught her lower lip between her teeth.

Josh wanted to be the one taking that bite.

"My turn," Casey said. "Only fair, right?"

Absolutely.

"I'm not looking for easy. I'm looking for someone who wants me so much that he can't hold back. That he won't hold back. I want us to both get lost— so lost we forget to come up for air. I don't want you treating me like a victim. I don't want you pulling back when the light of dawn is here. I'll never be anyone's dirty little secret, and I don't expect you to be mine, either. I want you—and I have, even before that crazy jerk abducted me. So this isn't about fear or adrenaline or anything like that. I wanted to kiss you when we were on that motorcycle. I wanted to see where the desire would go."

He knew exactly where it would go.

"So I guess…we have a deal?" She held out her hand and gave a little, self-conscious laugh. "This seems so odd. I mean, where's the romance and—"

His fingers curled around hers. "No deal."

Her eyes widened.

"Pleasure, sweetheart. What we have is a whole lot of pleasure." *And no regrets.* He used his grip on her hand to pull her closer. He'd known what would happen if he got his hands on her, and now, he wouldn't be letting her go.

His mouth took hers. A careful kiss, at first. Then he caught her lower lip between his teeth. He nibbled, he sucked and he gave in to the need he'd been feeling. Then he was kissing her, harder, deeper, letting go of his control. As she'd said...no holding back.

She gave a little moan in the back of her throat, and that husky sound just amped up his desire. He wanted to make her moan again. He wanted to make her scream. He wanted to make her go wild, as wild as he planned to get.

He pinned her against the door with his body. His hands caught hers and he curled his fingers around her wrists. He pushed her hands back against the wood as his mouth trailed down her neck. That little moan came again and he knew that he'd found her sweet spot. He licked and kissed, enjoying the way her body arched up against him. His arousal shoved against the front of his pants. His need was quick and fierce, but Josh was determined to take his time. To explore every inch of her. Some things shouldn't be rushed. Some people should be savored.

Casey should be savored.

He pulled back so that he could stare into her eyes.

The desire he saw there was like a punch straight to his gut. Did the woman have any idea what she was doing to him?

He let her hands go and she immediately reached for him. She grabbed his shirt and yanked and he was pretty sure buttons went flying. Josh blinked at her.

She smiled. The sexiest smile he'd ever seen.

"I told you." Her voice was the softest temptation. "I didn't do easy, either. Give me everything that you've got, Josh. I can handle it."

No doubt.

Her fingers slid down his chest, skating over his abs and down to his stomach. She touched the button on his pants—

He caught her hand. "I get to take care of you first."

She smiled. Again…he was lost.

Josh scooped Casey up into his arms. She was so light. Her scent surrounded him as he carried her to the bedroom—not her room, but his. He put her on her feet near his bed, and then he stripped her. Carefully. He started with her T-shirt. He pulled it over her head, making sure not to so much as jar her injuries. Then she was clad in her bra and her jeans. She'd kicked off her shoes, he wasn't sure where they were, and his fingers went to the snap of her jeans. In seconds, he was shoving those jeans down her legs, revealing the black panties that matched her bra. Sexy. So insanely sexy. Her breasts thrust against the cups of the bra. The panties barely shielded her secrets...

And he was about to explode.

Josh lowered her onto the bed and he followed her. His fingers slid over her, touching, stroking, driving her to a fever pitch. Then his mouth followed his fingers. He shoved the bra out of the way and kissed her breasts, loving her tight nipples. *Sweeter than candy.* He hadn't even realized he had a sweet tooth, not until that moment. He was sure he'd always crave her taste now.

He reached between her legs, felt her sexy core. Her nails sank into his shirt—he was still dressed. He'd ditched his shoes, but he still wore his pants and his shirt hung open.

"Get rid of your clothes," Casey said. "I want to feel you, *all* of you."

He'd give her exactly what she wanted.

He shrugged out of his shirt and tossed it across the room. He stood at the edge of the bed, moving away from her just long enough to strip. She watched him, her gaze drifting over his body and he wondered what she saw... He had scars. Scars from bullet wounds he'd taken while protecting his country. Scars from attacks he'd survived while being in the FBI. His body was rough, hard, and she was soft and silky. She was sensual, his every fantasy—and he hadn't even realized he'd been fantasizing about her. She was—

"You are so sexy," she murmured. Her hand reached

out to him. Then she was rising, moving to her knees and reaching for him. Her fingers slid over his chest and his muscles locked down. His arousal jerked toward her. Her fingers trailed over his nipples and then her head bent. She licked his nipple, she sucked, and her hair slid over his skin. His hands curled around her shoulders, the desire beat in his blood and then Josh tumbled her back on the bed.

Can't wait. Need her. Want her. Take her.

She gave a little laugh and his heart lurched. He grabbed the protection from his nightstand drawer before he went back to her. Her legs parted. She reached up to him—

No going back. No pretending this didn't happen in the morning. She'd never forget what they did this night. Neither would he.

Josh drove into her. He sank deep, then stilled for a moment as he stared into her eyes. Her gaze had gone even darker. Her cheeks were a rosy pink. She lifted her hips.

"Give me more."

He did. Josh withdrew, then thrust. His hips jerked against her. He lifted her up, then surged down, knowing he'd stroke across her most sensitive spot. She gave another moan, but that wasn't enough for him. Not nearly enough. His fingers pushed between them. Even as he thrust, he found the spot he wanted. He caressed and stroked until she came apart for him.

He loved the sound of her scream.

Josh followed her, driving harder, his pace nearly

frantic now. Again and again, he sank into her. The bed squeaked beneath them, his breath heaved from his lungs, and then the pleasure hit—crashing over him and obliterating everything else.

Only Casey.

Only Casey mattered.

HER EYES OPENED in the darkness. Casey's heart was racing, and fear held her in a tight grip. She lifted up her hands, afraid that she'd find them tied together with rough rope.

But her hands were free. She was free.

She just wasn't alone.

She could feel him against her body. They were still in his bed. She was still naked. Casey bet Josh was, too. They'd fallen asleep together. She couldn't remember the last time she'd stayed with a lover.

Part of her wanted to slip away right then, to go back to her bedroom. Another part of her wanted to stay exactly where she was. But…

What had woken her?

Then she heard the sound again—a vibration that pulsed. Quietly. From the floor? She slipped from the bed, trying hard not to wake Josh. She pulled a sheet with her, curling it around her body. The lights were out, but now that she was at the side of the bed, she could see a glow on the floor.

Her phone? Yes, it was the phone that Tom had given her. Vibrating. Ringing. So low and quiet— she picked it up and her finger slid across the screen.

"Hello?" Her voice was hushed.

"Casey?" Tom demanded. "Casey, what's wrong?"

Nothing. I'm just trying to be quiet so I don't wake my lover. "This isn't a good time." What time was it? Had to be nearing midnight. Why was Tom calling her so late? She edged toward the bathroom, still keeping her voice whisper-soft. She opened the door, eased inside and then shut that door firmly behind her. She hadn't woken Josh, at least, she didn't think she had.

"You didn't call me."

What? Seriously?

"I was worried," Tom continued, and he actually did sound worried. "I'm outside the sheriff's station. They just brought in Kurt Anderson."

Her heart jerked.

"They sneaked him in through the back door. They think no one knows what they're doing, but after your little visit to the prison today, Katrina and I were on stakeout here. We got footage of him going into the station. Now I'm going to need you to go on-air in the morning—be here at dawn. We'll get the sheriff to talk. You can get some quote from that FBI buddy of yours—"

"He's not my buddy." He was her lover. She could still feel his touch on her body.

"Whatever," Tom growled. "Get him or Sheriff Black to give us a sound bite. Use Duvane to find out what Kurt Anderson is saying to the authorities. Is the guy guilty? Did they find evidence on him? You're the star reporter—break this case like I know you can."

It was one thing to report on the story. It was another thing to wake up, hands and feet tied, as a madman in a mask prepared to slice you with his knife. "I'm not using Josh." She wanted to be clear on that. "It's not happening."

"Are you kidding me? Work that Casey Quinn charm on him—the way you always use it on those law enforcement guys. You can get him to tell you anything."

She didn't speak. Had she just heard a rustle of sound from the bedroom? Was Josh awake? Was he listening? *I won't use him.*

"I get that you're going through a lot." His tone had changed. That was Tom. Always working the angles. Now he sounded sympathetic. "And if you can't handle this story—if you're too close now—I can bring someone else in."

Ah, his ultimate threat—replace her. He'd tried that technique in the past. With her. With other reporters. That was the nature of the beast—in their business, there was always someone younger and hungrier waiting in the wings.

"I can do that," he continued carefully, "but I don't want to do it. I want you, Casey. You're my star. You're the one the public wants to see. Come back to me. Do this story like I know you can. I mean, seriously, this is *the* story of your career. You were a victim, so you'd be covering the case from an angle no one else could match. This would make us both."

She heard a creak from behind the door. Her shoulders stiffened. "I have to go."

"Casey." Worry sharpened Tom's tone. "Casey, are you okay?"

"I'm fine. It's just the middle of the night, and I'm going back to bed." It was easy to lie—to Tom, anyway.

"Be there at dawn. Katrina and I will be waiting for you at the station."

He hung up.

She exhaled slowly and opened the door. She expected Josh to be standing right there—only he wasn't. She inched forward, but Casey didn't see him in bed, either. "Josh?"

The bedroom door was open. She put the phone down on the nightstand and slipped out of the bedroom. She padded down the hallway and found him in the den—standing in front of those big glass windows. He stared out at the darkness.

"Glad to know you aren't using me."

He *had* heard that part. "Eavesdropping at bathroom doors, huh?" She swallowed. "I didn't mean to wake you."

He turned toward her. She realized that she was still just wearing the sheet. She'd hurried after him and dragged it with her. Maybe she should have stopped to grab a robe or something.

He was wearing a pair of loose sweatpants. They

hung low on his hips. A lamp was on near the sofa, spilling soft light into the room so that she could see him. *His disheveled hair.* She'd run her fingers through that hair. *The line of dark stubble on his jaw.* That stubble had rasped over her body. *His powerful build.* She'd touched every inch of him when they'd made love.

But he was standing there, his body stiff, his gaze locked on her. And something was just *off.*

"I can't figure you out."

She walked toward him and the thick carpeting swallowed her steps. "What's to figure out?" His voice had been tense, and she hated that. Hadn't they already covered the part where she said she *wouldn't* use him?

"I think you're a dangerous woman, Casey Quinn."

"That's only fair. I think you're a dangerous man."

His head inclined—in acknowledgment?

"That was Tom on the phone." Though she was betting he'd already figured out the identity of her caller. "He said that Sheriff Black and Agent Frost brought Kurt Anderson into the station. They sneaked him in through the back door. I thought you'd want to know—"

"I know. Tucker texted me earlier. You were asleep next to me, so I didn't wake you to tell you that they'd found him out on the water. They found him...and the boat he was on had an oil leak. Tucker smelled the oil all over the place."

Her heart lurched in her chest. "It's...him?"

He wasn't touching her. "We don't know that yet. The guy is drunk, way over the legal limit, so the sheriff brought him in for boating under the influence. That buys us time to question him, to thoroughly search the boat and to see just what secrets he's been hiding." His shoulders rolled back. "There's more, though. The guy…he had a bloody knife in the cabin on the boat. He said he'd cut himself while trying to slice through a tangled fishing wire."

"I stabbed my attacker." But she'd kept the knife, so there shouldn't be any bloody knife to find on Kurt's boat. Unless…

Unless he's already taken another victim.

Josh's head inclined. "All the angles are being investigated, I promise you that. And at first light, I'm going out. Tucker has pulled up all the GPS data from the boat Kurt used. I'm going diving to check out all the stops he's made. Just in case…" His words trailed away.

"In case there's another victim out there?" In case he'd grabbed someone else after Casey had gotten away.

"Just in case," he said flatly.

Her hands clenched around the sheet she wore, sinking into the material. "I'm guessing all of this is off the record?"

"This is for you to know…because you've got the biggest stake in this case. As far as the public and the press are concerned, the FBI and the local authorities are investigating a person of interest in the investigation. If we find evidence to conclusively link Kurt to the crime, we'll immediately call a press conference."

"You trust me to keep this quiet?"

He laughed, and the sound was a deep rumble. "Yeah, I actually *do* trust you, Casey."

That made her feel…warm. Good. "I trust you, too." As soon as the words slipped out, she felt her eyes widen. She hadn't meant to say that, had she? No, no, it was just… She cleared her throat. "You're FBI. Your whole bit is that you uphold the law and you keep the world safe. If I can't trust you, then I really can't trust anyone, can I?" Though wasn't that the way she'd played it for years, never trusting anyone? Always worrying, always being afraid? And what had playing it safe really gotten her?

She'd still been attacked again.

But I got away. I fought back.

"You should go back to sleep," Josh said, his voice still a dark rumble. "You've been through a lot, and you need to rest."

That was one idea. Certainly. Rest. He seemed to like that idea because he pushed it to her a lot. She nodded and turned away from him. She could feel Josh's gaze on her. Casey paced toward the couch, and then she turned off the light. Instantly, the room plunged into darkness.

"Casey?"

She let the sheet fall to the floor. "I don't want to rest." She turned back toward him. He still stood in front of that floor-to-ceiling window. He was a dark shadow and behind him, she could see the glittering stars. So many stars. "I want you." Because she could feel them running out of time. If he and Tucker found evidence to tie Kurt Anderson to the crimes, it would be great—they'd lock the killer away.

And then she'd report on the story and fly back home.

Josh would tie up loose ends and he'd head off to tackle another case.

The thought made her feel lost, sad. And she didn't want to face what was coming—not yet. Dawn would be there soon enough. She wanted to stay in the moment—with him. She wanted to hold the night close and pretend that nothing bad was waiting.

Just the moment. Just them.

She lifted her hands and pressed her body to him. Casey rose on her toes and her mouth brushed across his throat. She wasn't the only one with a sensitive spot. His hands clamped around her hips as he gave a ragged groan.

"Casey…"

"It's okay, being up here, near the windows…it's dark inside and only the ocean is out there to see us." She wanted him right there—then and there. She gave him a little nip and her hands slid down his chest. He was built—she loved his muscles. His strength and his heat. Loved the way he surrounded her and the way he made her *feel*.

She—

He lifted her up, holding her easily, and Casey gave a little laugh as her legs wrapped around his hips. His desire pressed against her. He wanted her just as much as she wanted him. Right there. Right then. As if nothing else mattered.

In that moment, nothing else did.

He kissed her, and she savored him. Her breasts pressed to his chest, his hands curled around her hips, and he turned, not pressing her to the glass of the window, but instead pushing her back against the wall to the right. He held her there, using his easy strength, kissing her and driving her out of her mind.

They could have built passion up slowly—with the sensual foreplay he'd shown her before. But Casey wasn't in the mood for slow. She wasn't in the mood for anything but him.

"Now," Casey whispered. "Right now."

His hand eased between their bodies. He stroked her and had her gasping and arching toward him. His fingers slid into her. Casey's eyes squeezed closed. He knew just how to touch her, exactly what she wanted, as if they'd been lovers for years instead of—

Just one night.

He caressed the center of her need—the spot that made her gasp again and press harder to him. His fingers filled her and her whole body shuddered as the first wave of release hit her.

"So beautiful," he rasped.

Her breath heaved out of her chest.

He kissed her again, softly, and, still holding her tightly, he went back into the bedroom. He put her on the bed, and she heard the rustle as he grabbed for the protection. He returned to her seconds later, and she was the one to push him down so that he lay on the bed. Casey rose above him, her knees on either side of his hips. She lowered herself onto him, and he filled her so completely. When he was fully inside her, she stilled. In the darkness, she tried to see his eyes.

She wanted to see him.

But his fierce hold lifted her up, and she sank back down onto him. The passion swept through her and she could only move, faster, rougher, and her hands slammed against his chest. Nothing else mattered— just them. Just that moment.

Again and again, her body lifted and her hips pushed back down on him.

The pleasure hit her, a climax so intense that her whole body was engulfed by the release, and he was moving—tumbling her onto her back, thrusting deep and then exploding within her.

In the aftermath, the only sound was their ragged breathing.

And...

He kissed her.

IT WASN'T OVER. The cops and the FBI might think they were so smart, but they had no clue. They weren't going to defeat him. He'd been too careful.

There was no evidence, nothing to tie him to any of the crimes.

They didn't have their killer. They wouldn't have him.

They'd look ridiculous in front of the media. They'd turn up *nothing*.

And he would continue his hunt.

He knew exactly where Casey Quinn was hiding. Did she think that she was safe? That she'd gotten away from him? No, no, she'd just made him angrier.

It was time to finish what he'd started. This time, she wouldn't slip away.

This time, she'd be the one who bled.

She wasn't going to end this tale as a survivor. That wasn't the way she got to escape. That wasn't her final story.

She'd be a victim. A footnote. And he'd be the lead.

Chapter Ten

"Why the hell am I here?" Kurt Anderson let out a loud, long groan. "And why does my head feel like a jackhammer is inside it?" He sat up, hunching on the cot in the jail cell—the holding cell was in the back of the sheriff's station.

Josh slanted a glance at Tucker. The other FBI agent stood just a few feet away from him. They were both outside the cell, ready to see just what Kurt had to say. Dawn had finally come to Hope. Josh had stopped at the sheriff's station so that he could check in with Tucker before he went out on the water to begin searching.

Tucker's gaze was considering as it swept over the prisoner. Did the guy buy Kurt as the killer they were after?

"You're here," Tucker explained quietly, "because last night when Sheriff Black and I approached you on your rented vessel, you were so stinking drunk you could barely walk, much less drive a boat. So we brought you in both for your safety and for everyone else's. That whole stinking drunk bit? That's also why you feel as if a jackhammer is going off in your head."

Kurt squinted at him. "Do I know you?" His squinty gaze darted to Josh. "You both look liked Feds."

"We are Feds," Josh answered. "And, yeah, you know me. I'm Agent Josh Duvane." He inclined his head toward Tucker. "And this is Special Agent Tucker Frost." He paused for a moment. "And we need to discuss something your father recently said."

At that magic word, *father*, Kurt's whole face hardened. "I've already talked to so many suits about him… Questions come constantly. For the last time—" he surged off the cot and lurched toward the bars, his face twisted in angry lines "—I didn't know what that sick freak was doing. I had no idea that he'd killed my sister. I had no idea that he'd hurt anyone. I wasn't a part of anything that he'd done—"

"We actually aren't here to talk to you about what *he* did," Tucker interrupted smoothly. "His actions are his own. It's you that we want to talk about."

Kurt was pale, but two angry splotches of color appeared on his cheeks. "Me? You want to talk about me?"

"You are aware of the recent murders in this town, correct?" Tucker pushed.

Kurt blinked.

"Kylie Shane, Bridget Donaldson and Tonya Myers," Josh supplied curtly.

"Right, yeah, so what?" Then Kurt shook his head. "Wait, I don't mean that. I mean...what do their deaths have to do with me?"

"Your father said you were responsible for those crimes." Josh delivered this news quietly.

Kurt's jaw dropped. *"What?"*

"Do you know Casey Quinn?" Tucker asked. It was an old technique—keep firing at the suspect, keep him off guard. If they both went in with questions, the guy would be confused. And he might slip up.

"Casey—the reporter? Yeah, yeah, I know her. I talked to her a few times. She's not like the others—she wanted to tell *my* side and—" He stopped. "She was taken. I—I saw that on the news."

"Casey stabbed the man who abducted her." Tucker pointed to the guy's arm. "Can't help but notice that ragged cut you've got there."

"I cut myself trying to untangle stupid fishing wire!" Those dark spots of color on Kurt's cheeks darkened. "I'm not the killer! I didn't hurt those women! I haven't hurt *anyone*!" Then he gave a ragged laugh. "Though I wanted to hurt someone... I wanted to kill my old man. I wanted to wipe him off the face of the earth. I didn't. Hayden stopped me. Said I was better than my father..." Again, that ragged laughter came. "If only he knew..."

Josh didn't look away from the man before him. "Knew what—exactly?"

Kurt swallowed. His hands rose and curled around the bars. "I want out of here."

"What is it that you wish Hayden Black knew?" Tucker's gaze was fixed on the prisoner.

"Don't I get a lawyer or something?" Kurt's confusion that he'd suffered after waking was vanishing. "I want a lawyer. I want out of here. And I don't care what kind of BS story my crazy father is telling you—I didn't hurt those women. I wouldn't do that. *I'm not him.*"

Tucker took a step back from the bars. "We'll get you that lawyer." He jerked his head toward Josh. "Let's go." He turned on his heel, marching away.

"I wouldn't do that!" Kurt yelled after him.

Josh stared at the prisoner a moment longer, then he turned and followed his friend out of the holding area. As soon as they were clear, Tucker stopped. He stared straight ahead.

"Uh, buddy?" Josh gazed at him with worry. "You okay?"

Tucker glanced back at him. "I want him to be telling the truth."

Josh wasn't so sure the guy *was* telling the truth, though, and—

"I want it for personal reasons. I want it because— damn, just because you have a killer in the family, it doesn't mean you're screwed to hell and back, too, right? We can be different." He blew out a hard breath and shook his head. "I'm losing my perspective on this case. This one was supposed to be my proving ground, and I'm letting my own past blind me."

"Why'd the father point the finger at him?" Josh demanded. "Why shove the guy down our throats? Because nothing I know about Theodore Anderson indicates the guy is the kind, concerned citizen type."

"No, he isn't concerned. He was all too ready to throw his son under the bus."

"Considering that Kurt had to be persuaded by the sheriff not to kill his father, I'm guessing it's clear their relationship is shot to hell and back. So maybe the father had decided to get a little last-minute revenge by trying to take his son's freedom away."

"We need evidence." Tucker's chin notched up. "You ready to dive?"

"Always."

They filed out of the hallway and headed back to the sheriff's office. Casey was in there, sitting across from Hayden. When Josh opened the door to the office, she immediately jumped to her feet and came toward him.

Why did that make him feel good? No, *she* made him feel good.

And that could be dangerous. *Be careful with her.* Josh knew he had to tread very, very carefully. "The guy wants a lawyer," he said, making sure his voice was flat. "Kurt isn't going to talk anymore. He's done. And I'm heading out with my team for the dives." He knew he'd be diving for most of the day, and he hated to leave Casey on her own. He'd tried to convince her to stay at the penthouse. Local FBI agents would have been there to protect her in his absence but...

She'd been adamant. She wasn't going to hide, not anymore. His promised twenty-four hours weren't even up. But he couldn't *force* her back into protection. At least, not yet he couldn't.

"There have been no missing persons cases filed lately," Hayden said as he rose from his chair. "And the perp we're after—he always calls to tell us when he has a victim. The guy acts like it is some kind of game. Can we find him before the victim dies? That's his taunt."

Casey flinched. "Only the game didn't work out the way he expected last time."

No, it hadn't.

"If he picked another victim with no close ties, then it's possible her disappearance just hasn't been reported." Josh couldn't overlook that possibility. "So I'll dive down to every spot on that boat's navigation record. If a victim is there, I'll find her." His gaze slid back to Casey. Before he left, he needed to know that she was safe. He needed to know—

There was as sharp knock at the door behind him. He glanced back and saw Deputy Finn Patrick open the door. Finn's face showed his worry. "Sheriff Black, the reporters are out front again. They got tipped off that we may have a suspect in custody."

"And the circus never ends," Hayden muttered. "Thanks, Finn, I'll handle them."

But Finn didn't leave. His stare shifted to Casey. "Guy out there...said he's her producer. He's demanding to see Ms. Quinn."

"He can demand all he wants," Hayden began, "I don't—"

"I'll handle him." Her voice was soft. Her stare was certain. "My producer, my job. I've got this." She started to walk toward Finn, but Josh stepped into her path.

His hand curled around her shoulder. "Are you sure about this?" Sure that she wanted to give up federal protection? Sure that she wanted to walk back into the fire?

"I know Tom. By now, he'll have bodyguards for me. I'll be protected. And you...you and the other agents have other things to do. You can't watch me forever."

But he wanted to.

His hand fell away.

There was so much more he wanted to say to Casey, but with everyone else watching them...he just let her go. Josh watched as she walked away.

"It's hard when emotions get involved," Hayden said quietly, and Josh wondered just how much he'd already given away. He looked back at the sheriff, but Hayden wasn't staring at him. He was looking at a framed photo on his desk. "I'm glad Jill is out of town right now. Going through all of this again— seeing Kurt brought in for questions relating to all these murders—it would just stir up the pain from her past again." His jaw locked. "And I can't stand to see Jill's pain."

Jill West worked on the FBI's Child Abduction Rapid Deployment Team—and Josh knew she'd taken that job because of her own painful past. Jill was currently training a new crop of agents up in Quantico, and, like Hayden, he thought that might be for the best.

"When emotions are involved," Hayden continued and his gaze lifted from the photo to lock on Josh. "You can lose perspective and that loss can lead to deadly consequences."

Josh didn't intend to lose *anything*. "I need to check in with my team. We've got a lot of work to do on the water."

Tucker followed him out, and they stopped near the check-in desk to go over their files. He caught a glimpse of Casey—she'd paused right before the glass doors that would take her out of the station.

She looked back at him. She gave him a smile that made his chest ache, then she opened the door and stepped outside. He saw Tom's face as the guy rushed toward her. Katrina was there. A half-dozen other reporters closed in on Casey.

"We could have forced her to stay in custody," Tucker said, his voice careful.

If only. But things were more complex than they seemed. "I got word from the FBI brass that we had to let her go." He hadn't told Casey about that, not yet. "Seems her *producer* has some powerful friends, and he didn't like the way we were 'imprisoning' his reporter."

Tucker swore.

"Yeah, exactly how I feel. Tom promised she'd have the best bodyguards on her while she was still down here. And I was told that unless we wanted a media relations nightmare on our hands, then Casey got to walk."

And she'd just walked away.

His fingers drummed on the countertop. He couldn't see her any longer.

"Things between you two…they got personal, didn't they?"

Did *everyone* notice? "She was a victim." He straightened his shoulders. Finn was nearby, watching and listening too closely. "And I'm the guy who needs to dive into the water. You coming on the boat?"

"Yeah, yeah, I'll be right with you."

Time to get back to business.

Tom had better hold up his end of the deal. He'd better keep those guards on Casey. If he didn't…

If anything happens to Casey, I'll destroy him.

THE QUESTIONS WERE battering at her, nonstop. She'd been in a crowd of reporters, just like this one— too many times. Casey knew better than to try answering any of the barrage of questions being fired at her. She would handle the press her way, in her time. And right then…they weren't getting any comments from her.

Tom grabbed her hand and steered her toward the SUV that waited. It was a massive beast of a vehicle. She jumped into the back, and he followed behind her. Katrina jumped in the front passenger seat.

As soon as Casey got inside the vehicle, she saw that two men were already waiting there. A quiet, intense-looking African American male sat to the left. The driver—a redheaded guy—immediately took off as soon as they were all in the vehicle.

"Hello," Casey said to the man in the back with her.

He inclined his head. "Ms. Quinn."

"Just call me—"

"Didn't expect the full crowd to be there," Tom grumbled as he shoved in next to her. "Hard for us to get any footage when they were blocking the place. No matter, we'll come back and do the shots then. For now, we'll go to the beach—maybe down to the dock—and get some scene recordings there. You can tell your story while the waves pound behind you. Very moving…especially considering the other women were found in the gulf."

"Do you mean to be an unsympathetic jerk?"

He blinked. "What?"

"Do you mean to come across that way…or do you just not even hear the words coming out of your mouth?"

He blinked again.

There was a smothered laugh from the driver.

Tom's eyes narrowed. "Did you seriously just speak to your boss that way?"

"Yes, I did. And did you seriously just act as if those victims were props to use in your video footage?"

His lips compressed.

"Ah…Casey, it's good to have you back," Katrina said.

Casey's gaze slid to her. Katrina had turned to give her a weak smile.

"Have you met your protection? That's Andrew to your left."

"Just call me Drew," the guy rumbled.

"And you call me Casey."

Katrina pointed to the driver. "That's Shamus. They both came very highly recommended."

"We'll be your shadows," Drew told her. "You won't have to worry about a thing. We guarantee your safety."

If Kurt Anderson was the killer, then she didn't have to worry—he was locked up. Everyone would be safe again. But if he wasn't the perp…

Then the man who wants me dead is still out there.

"So…DO YOU think he was dumping bodies out there?" Chaz Fontel shook his head. A tribal tattoo circled his upper arm and his long hair brushed across the collar of his shirt. "I can't believe that guy—I mean, I felt *sorry* for him, you know?"

Chaz was the owner of the boat rental shop, and

he was also the guy who seemed more than eager to cooperate with the Feds. He'd already provided them with all the information they needed to go back and retrace all the stops that Kurt Anderson had made on his trips.

And the guy had made a *lot* of trips. But none of the trips taken from the boat he'd used matched up with the spots where they'd found their other three victims.

Did that mean Kurt was innocent? Or that he'd just used another vessel when he disposed of the bodies? Josh knew Tucker already had agents canvasing the other boat rental shops in the area, just in case Kurt *had* used another vessel. But he might not have rented another boat. Half the people in that town owned boats. He could have borrowed one, could have taken—

"Did Kurt Anderson ever say anything to you about his father's crimes?" Tucker asked.

Chaz gave a low whistle. "No, man, and it's not like I'd ask, you know? Talk about a painful subject. I just rented him the boat. That's it."

A dark SUV pulled up near the dock. Josh's gaze narrowed as the doors to that vehicle opened.

Katrina. Tom.

Casey...

He stiffened.

He saw the two guys who exited the vehicle, too, and instantly pegged them as the protection that she'd been promised.

"Oh, man, is that Casey Quinn?" Chaz asked, excitement in his tone. "I love her."

Josh's gaze cut back to him, but Chaz wasn't paying him—or Tucker—any attention. His focus was entirely on Casey.

"Heard about what happened to her." Chaz's hands fisted. "So glad she's okay. I watch her all the time."

"Do you now…" Josh muttered. Not a question.

"Maybe she'll want to interview me." Chaz's shoulders straightened. "I mean, I'm the one who rented Kurt the boat. Bet she'll want to talk to me. I bet—"

Josh stepped in front of the guy, blocking his view of Casey. "We're talking to you right now."

"Uh, yeah. Right. He, uh, never mentioned his old man. Never mentioned anything. Just came on board with his gear—his bags and the coolers and he left. Figured the guy just wanted some time by himself. Water can heal the soul, you know? That's what the ocean does."

It healed—or the ocean became a grave for the dead.

Josh cast one last look over at Casey. He found her staring back at him.

"YOUR AGENT IS going out on the water?" Katrina sidled closer to Casey and kept her voice low. "What is he trying to find out there?"

Casey tried to drag her eyes off Josh. Why was she reacting this way to him? "USERT is his primary job with the FBI. You know that."

"Yeah, but I mean…who is he going to rescue down there? Is another victim in the water?"

"USERT stands for Underwater Search *and* Evidence Response Team. He's searching." For clues. For evidence.

And, yes, for a body. But she really hoped he didn't find one.

Tom was talking to the two men who were her new guards.

"If he's USERT, then why did he spend so much time looking after you?" Katrina wanted to know. "Weren't there other agents—"

"They didn't need him in the water then. So he thought it would be good for me to have an agent… with me."

"Hmm."

What was that supposed to mean?

Katrina smiled at her. "I think he likes you."

I think I like him. "He was doing his job. With this many agents in the area, everyone is assigned a task. I was his task."

Katrina lifted a brow. "You really think you were just a task to him?"

She hoped that she'd been more but…

He was climbing onto a boat. Pulling tanks on after him. She knew he'd be heading out for his dive. When he got back, would he come and find her?

Should she find him?

"I can keep a secret, you know," Katrina added. Her voice had become even softer. "You…you fell for the agent, didn't you? I mean, I've worked with you a long time, and I've never seen you look at anyone the way you're looking at him right now."

"We just met." She tried to brush Katrina's words aside even though she knew she'd given too much away. *The way you're looking at him right now.* "He was doing his job. And I was barely holding things together."

"Let's get her wired up!" Tom called out.

Tom, ready for business. She needed to get ready, too. This *was* her job, after all.

Casey squared her shoulders. The waves crashed behind her.

HE LEFT THE wet suit at his waist. Josh would finish getting it into position when they were closer to the first dive site. The boat shot away from the dock, and his gaze once more slid to Casey. He could barely see her now.

"You think we can trust her?" Tucker asked him. "Just how much did you share with her while they two of you were in that penthouse?"

Josh turned his head and met the other man's gaze. "I trust her."

"She's a reporter, going live right now from the looks of things. If she reveals too much—"

"She won't."

"For both our sakes, I hope so." Tucker wasn't wearing a dive suit. Josh and his team were going down, but Tucker was staying on the boat. The water splashed around them as they flew across the waves.

"Do you think there's another victim out there?" Josh asked Tucker.

His friend's jaw hardened. "If there isn't—" he rolled back his shoulders "—I'm afraid there will be one very, very soon."

That was Josh's fear, too.

They didn't speak again, not until they were at the first dive site. Josh pulled his wet suit into position. He secured his mask and slid the tank on his back. He had his dive knife ready—the way he always did. He *never* went down without a dive knife strapped to his ankle. He'd once had to use his knife on a blacktip shark that had gotten too curious—and aggressive. He checked his BCD. The buoyancy control device was absolutely essential for diving. He put his mouthpiece in, then sat on the edge of the boat. Two of his team members were in position near him. Josh put his thumb and forefinger together in the Okay signal, and then he fell backward, tumbling into the water below.

"CASEY! *CASEY QUINN!*"

She turned at the shout. She'd just finished her first segment. Tom was a few feet away, Katrina was filming and her guards—they sure tensed fast at that yell.

A man with sun-streaked hair jogged toward her. He was waving.

Her guards immediately moved to intercept him.

"Hey, no, wait! I'm a witness! I think Casey wants to talk with me!"

"A witness?" Tom's brows shot up. "Let the guy through."

The two guards hesitated. Especially Drew. He looked seriously unhappy, but he finally stepped back.

And Casey got a good look at the guy approaching her. He had a tribal tattoo around his upper arm. A golden tan was on his body and he wore a T-shirt with Chaz's Rentals on the front.

"Just talked to the FBI." His chest puffed out. "Thought you might want to talk to me, too."

He was the boat rental manager. Right.

"Chaz Fontel," he said, offering her his hand. "I'm a *big* fan, Casey."

Her fingers curled around his. She looked down and saw his wrist—a strong wrist. Tanned.

For an instant, she was back in that cabin, tied up, and her attacker's glove had come down just enough for her to see his wrist…

"I'm so sorry you were hurt."

Her gaze slid back up to his face. Sympathy was there but…his eyes seemed a little too bright. *He's excited.* Excited because he'd been working with the FBI? Because he thought he was helping to crack the case or—

"They're looking for bodies." His voice was a whisper. Chaz still hadn't let go of her hand. "More women, lost beneath the waves." He was still holding her hand. "Such a crying shame. For something so beautiful...to just become a grave."

A chill skated down her spine. She pulled her hand away from Chaz and backed up a step. Her shoulder bumped into Drew's. Immediately, he was pushing her behind him and putting himself between her and Chaz.

"Hold on!" Tom's voice called out. "I think we need to hear more from Mr. Fontel."

Chaz glanced at him, frowning. "What do you want to hear?"

Tom smiled at him. He motioned for Katrina to get her camera filming. "Everything."

Chapter Eleven

He hit pay dirt at the second dive site. Josh saw the bag, a big, thick, black bag that had been weighed down and tossed into the water. It had sunk to the bottom, hit the sand and stayed trapped there.

It was a large bag—easily big enough to cover a body. And it was long—bulky with its contents.

He didn't want a woman to be in that bag.

His team worked as bubbles drifted up from their tanks. They were trying to protect the evidence, not destroy anything. The bag was heavy—*so heavy that a victim could be inside*. His thoughts stayed dark as they worked.

He was too used to finding the dead.

It took time, but Josh and his crew got the bag back to the boat. Water streamed from it as they set the bag on the deck. Josh dropped his equipment. He stored his tank.

Then the team gathered around that bag.

Josh exhaled as he pulled out his dive knife. He

cut through the hemp rope that bound the top of the bag, and the bag opened. He reached inside and—

His fingers touched something soft.

Damn it.

CASEY WAS WAITING at the station when Josh came back with his team. Her guards were with her—they'd stayed close all day long. And when she saw Josh's team head to the back of the station, she knew something big had happened.

"Did they find another body?" Katrina whispered. "Is that what happened?"

There was only one way to find out. Other reporters were at the front of the station. She'd been staying out of their line of sight. She'd given a few other interviews during the day—enough to make most of those reporters happy, but she hadn't wanted to tempt fate by staying right in the mix with them.

"Did someone die in your place?" Katrina asked.

And Casey was chilled to the bone.

KURT ANDERSON HADN'T been released from custody. He was still at the station, only now his lawyer, Sarah Hastings, was at his side.

"My client has been held here entirely too long," she began as soon as Tucker and Josh stepped into the little conference room. The sheriff was already in there, his shoulders against the wall on the right. "He was brought in under a charge of boating under the influence but—"

"We found your bag," Josh cut in.

The woman frowned. "Bag? What bag?" Then she waved a hand dismissively. "You have no idea that anything you *may* have found is linked to my client in any—"

Josh pulled out an evidence bag and placed it on the table right in front of Kurt. "Does that look familiar to you?"

Kurt's shoulders hunched. A pink bear was in that plastic bag…a bear that was still soaking wet.

"Because we found that bear—and dolls and toys and clothes—at the bottom of the Gulf."

Kurt reached for the bag, but Tucker scooped it up before he could touch it.

"You're not supposed to have it," Kurt whispered. "I was giving it back to her." His Adam's apple bobbed as he swallowed. "Do you know…he kept everything…?"

"Stop taking, Kurt," his lawyer advised him sharply. *"Stop."*

But he just shook his head. "Her room was like a shrine. Her books were on her desk, and her clothes still hung in her closet. Stuffed animals—the ones she'd had when she was four and five—they were still in her closet. He kept everything, like it all mattered. Like she mattered. When all that time, he'd been the one to kill her."

Sarah shot to her feet. "All my client did was dispose of items that were no longer wanted at his home.

So there *could* be an illegal dumping charge, but given the situation—"

"After his arrest, the cops and Feds took some stuff from Christy's rooms, but I didn't know what to do with the rest of her things. Christy always loved the water, so I took it all out there." He was staring at his fisted hands. "I let it sink. I told her goodbye."

Sarah's hand curled around his shoulder. "You don't need to answer any of their questions. They're just trying to trip you up. They're trying to pin *murders* on you, and you haven't done anything wrong." Her eyes glinted. "My client is grief stricken. He is trying to get through each day the best way that he can. So, yes, maybe he had too much to drink. That's on him. But he hasn't hurt anyone. He *isn't* his father, and this interview? It's over." She nodded once, decisively. "So either charge my client with something *other* than boating under the influence—or this illegal dumping joke—or let him walk. Because I think he's been through more than enough."

They didn't have any evidence to tie him to the murders. And the way the guy was shaking, the way he'd gone solid white when he saw that little stuffed animal, Josh wasn't so sure that Kurt was the killer they were after.

Kurt's father had killed his own daughter. It wasn't beyond the realm of possibility that he wanted to destroy his son's life, too. And a false allegation had been all it took to put Kurt under the microscope.

"He can go," Hayden said. "But...don't leave town, Kurt, okay? There will be more questions."

Not that there *could* be more questions. Just that there *will* be more.

Sarah kept her arm around Kurt as they headed out of the room. She was whispering to him, her voice oddly soothing. Her pose with him was almost... intimate.

The door closed quietly behind them.

"I don't want it to be him," Hayden said quietly. He raked a hand over his face. "I knew him when we were kids. The things his father did...the things he tried to do to my Jill—I hate Theodore Anderson for that. *But I don't want Kurt to be like him.*"

"Maybe he isn't," Tucker said. "But I still want to have eyes on him. Let's keep a tail behind the guy just so we know his movements."

Hayden nodded. "Already done. I gave the order right before I came in for this little sit-down."

Josh paced around the room. "If it's not Kurt Anderson, then we're back to square one. We need to take another look at our perp..."

"Male, Caucasian, fit," Tucker began as he ticked off the points they knew. "I'd say we're looking for an individual between twenty-five and thirty-five. He knows the area, and he knows his victims. By picking individuals who are all survivors, he's showing that he's done research on them. They aren't random. He's proving a point—"

"That no one can survive what he's done."

Tucker nodded. "Exactly. When Casey escaped, I wondered if the killer would immediately get another victim. Or if—"

"If he'd come after Casey again." Josh's body had tensed.

"But he didn't come after her," Hayden said. "And he hasn't taken anyone else, either."

He hasn't come after her yet. Josh wished Casey was still with him. He needed her close so that he could be sure she was safe.

He just... He wanted her close.

"Casey stabbed him," Hayden continued, his brows pulling low. "Is it possible that she stabbed him so deeply that the guy is still recovering? Is that why we haven't seen any action from him? Hell, maybe she even killed him."

"Not enough blood at the scene for that." Tucker had crossed his arms over his chest. "And I have the FBI techs doing a rush job on the blood we recovered from the knife she had. They're comparing it to the blood we took from the knife we found on Kurt's boat."

"If it's a match, we bring the guy right back in." Josh knew those tests took time, but he wanted the results yesterday. "Another reason to keep a guard on him. Until we know for sure, one way or another about the blood, he stays at the top of our suspect list." Josh considered what else they knew about the killer. "Our perp is organized. Meticulous. Such a careful planner. Maybe he is intending to go after

Casey again, but he has to wait. He has to pick his moment." Even as he spoke, his gut was clenching. "We had her in the penthouse, with top-of-the-line security. It could be that he just *couldn't* get to her there."

"She's not at the penthouse any longer," Hayden pointed out. His gaze was on Josh. "She's out in the open. That producer of hers had Casey filming for most of the day. Everyone could see her."

Josh's jaw hardened.

"She had guards with her. One of them, I recognized. Drew Pitch. He's an ex-Ranger. Hard-as-nails kind of guy. He'll keep an eye on her."

It wouldn't be the same, though, with Josh not being near her. Not watching out for her himself. "I'm going to talk to her." Just to make sure that nothing had happened that day that jarred her. Nothing that set off her suspicions. Letting her just walk away after what happened—yes, the FBI brass had said they couldn't force her to stay in protective custody, but Josh couldn't shake the feeling that she was just bait out in the open.

Tom Warren loved his flashy headlines. Would he use Casey, trying to attract a killer? To get the story of a lifetime?

Not on my watch.

"Look, there's Kurt Anderson!" Katrina called. "He's walking out of the station—that means they didn't have enough to charge him, right? I've got to get the footage." She rushed across the street.

Other reporters and cameramen had already closed in. Casey didn't move.

"Don't you want the story?" Tom asked her as he slid closer. He'd been doing that all day—getting too close. Touching her shoulder. Her arm. Hovering. Pressing. Smothering.

"Anderson isn't going to say anything right now. The woman with him—that's Sarah Hastings. She's his lawyer." Because Casey had met the woman when she'd first talked to Kurt. Their meeting had been set up—and moderated—by Sarah. "She's protective of him." Maybe even in love with him, judging by the way Casey had seen the other woman stare at Kurt. "She won't let anyone push her client right now."

Tom moved in front of her, blocking her view of the crowd. "You're coming back home with me."

"Excuse me?" Her brows rose. Her guards were just a few feet away.

"I've rented a house on the beach—there are plenty of rooms. It has great security. The guards will be close in case you need anything. If the perp comes for you, we'll all be ready."

If the perp comes... There was just something about the way he said those words. "Do you *want* him to come?"

His lips parted. "What? No, Casey, I want you safe." His hands curled around her shoulders. "You matter to me. Don't you realize how much?" His voice softened. "Maybe I didn't even realize how much, not until I heard that you'd been taken. Priorities—they have a way of becoming crystal clear in moments of danger. You think you have all the time in the world, and then—bam. You realize you could lose the thing that matters most."

Oh, no. This wasn't happening. "Tom...you're my boss."

"I could be more."

I don't want more. "I don't cross that line. I *won't* cross it." She didn't want him—had never been attracted to him that way. He could use his easy smiles on other women. They weren't for her. He wasn't for her.

She much preferred a man who moved with lethal grace, who gazed at her as if she were the only woman in any room. As if—

"Am I interrupting something?" Josh's voice. Low, drawling.

Angry?

Tom jerked back and his hands fell away from her body as he looked back to find Josh behind him. "Agent Duvane! I just— I didn't realize you were there."

Casey hadn't realized he was there, either. The guy was far too good at sneaking up on people.

"It's getting late," Josh said, inclining his head toward the setting sun. "Don't you think Casey should be off the streets?"

"I was just about to take her home," Tom replied stiffly. "But thanks for your concern, *Agent*—"

"An arrest hasn't been made. Anderson left with his lawyer."

"Yes." Tom's jaw was clenched. "We saw that."

"The FBI still has the penthouse, Casey. Your guards—" Josh motioned to the men near her. "They can watch you during the day. But you're welcome to continue staying at the safe house during the night. You know it's a secure location."

"She's coming with—" Tom began.

"I want to go back to the crime scene," Casey blurted.

Josh blinked. "What?"

"I didn't get to go back this morning, like we planned." She stepped closer to him, brushing past Tom. "We still have a little bit of daylight left. Will you take me back there now?" She'd remembered something at the hotel. Maybe she'd remember at the beach house, too. A tiny lead could make a big difference.

"Yeah, I'll take you." Josh's hand reached out and curled around hers and his touch just felt right. Warm. Strong. Safe.

"Casey!" Tom blustered. "I don't know—"

She turned her head to look at him and his words stopped. "You want the story, right? Agent Duvane can get me access to the crime scene. You can't. I'm going back. I'm doing this *my* way." Her gaze slid to the two guards. "Drew and Shamus, thank you for your help today. I won't be needing your services for the night, though. The night is covered." She wasn't staying at Tom's place. She was staying at the penthouse.

With Josh.

Tom's eyes narrowed. "That's your choice."

"Yes, it is. And we'd better hurry before that sun is gone." She didn't want to be at the scene after dusk.

She followed Josh back to the parking lot behind the station. Katrina saw her, frowned, but didn't speak. A few moments later, Josh was handing her a helmet.

Back to the motorcycle?

She didn't protest this time. Casey put the helmet on her head. She slid onto the bike behind Josh and she held on tight.

He revved the engine, but he didn't pull away. His body was tense, his muscles hard, and she heard him say, "I missed you today."

Casey smiled. In the midst of everything bad happening, he'd just made her feel good. "I missed you, too." She didn't know what that meant—for their future. For them. But...

It meant *something*.

The motorcycle roared away.

"So..." DREW SAID as he raised his brows. "That mean we're done for the night?"

Tom had his hands on his hips as he stared after

the motorcycle. "Yes, you're done. Both of you." Because he wouldn't be needing their services.

Shamus slapped his hand on Drew's shoulders. "Let's go get a drink, buddy."

Drew hesitated a moment, his gaze on Tom's face. "You sure she's good?"

"She's with an FBI agent," Katrina announced as she strode toward them. "How much better can she get?"

Drew nodded and headed off with Shamus. Tom kept staring after the motorcycle.

"Tom?" Katrina prodded. "You okay?"

"This is my story."

"Yes, I know."

"Casey doesn't get that." He shook his head. "Why doesn't she get that?"

Katrina didn't speak.

"I'm getting a drink." Then Tom stormed off down the street. He left Katrina behind him, standing alone.

CHAZ FONTEL CHECKED the lines on his boats. It was quitting time, and he wanted to make sure he stepped in early at the local bar. He'd been interviewed by Casey Quinn—and at least four other reporters that day. He needed to tell his friends about those reporters.

He also wanted to make sure he warned people to stay away from Kurt Anderson. The guy was *trouble*.

Chaz turned around. And he had to do a quick

double take when he saw someone standing less than five feet away. *"Jesus!"* He put his hand to his heart. "Didn't even see you there!" He laughed. "Look, this town is jumpy enough as it is. You can't go sneaking up on people." He approached his visitor. "You here to rent another boat? Because I was shutting down early today. I'm not going to do the night rentals for a while. I get that it's a good way to blow off steam, but in light of everything that's been happening, I just think a break is needed." He walked past the customer and moved toward his office. "Sorry, but I can't—"

The blow struck him in the back of the head. Hard and brutal, swinging down at him and sending him crashing onto the wooden dock. Then he was being kicked, again and again, and he rolled, trying to protect himself. He rolled—

And crashed right into the water. He tried to kick up, breaking through the surface, but—

As soon as his head cleared the water, he was hit. Something hard and wooden slammed into his head. An oar?

He went back down.

This time, he couldn't kick up.

JOSH BRAKED THE motorcycle just beyond the line of yellow police tape. The setting sun had turned the sky a dark red. The waves were crashing nearby.

Casey was still behind him, her hands wrapped tightly around his waist. It was so odd, but the woman just seemed to fit him. Inside and out. He kicked down the stand, and she slid back. He immediately missed her warmth.

He missed *her*.

"I thought it wouldn't seem as scary, coming here with you. But…it still does." She rubbed her upper arms, as if chilled in the summer air. "Let's go inside, okay? Waiting just makes me more nervous."

He caught her hand. Josh threaded his fingers with hers. Then he hurried forward. His shoes sank into the sand and he bent, sliding beneath the line of yellow police tape. The wind blew against them, flattening their clothes and tossing their hair. The house was built up on stilts, protecting it from the storm surge that could come if a hurricane ever turned toward Hope. They climbed those wooden steps slowly that led up to the structure. A temporary construction door was in place over the main entrance, a door that didn't have a lock. He pushed it open, and even though there was still muted light coming into the cabin, Josh pulled out his flashlight.

"Let's go up to the next level," Casey said. "Because the only thing I remember down here…is seeing you."

They started walking. Her phone rang. The cry was loud and peeling and she jumped. Casey fumbled and pulled out her phone. "Tom." His name was a sigh. "Give me just a second, okay?"

Josh waited. His light swung around the cabin. Construction had halted after the discovery that the place had been a crime scene. Would the builders eventually finish? Or would they rip the place down? Josh didn't exactly see anyone wanting to live in a serial killer's old lair.

Casey put the phone to her ear. "Hi, Tom…No, no, we're not at the penthouse yet. I told you that I wanted to stop by the crime scene…I'm *fine*…No, Tom, I don't need you. And if I remember anything else, I'm telling the FBI first, not you." Her voice was brisk. "Good night." She shoved the phone into the back pocket of her jeans.

Josh raised a brow. "Trouble?"

"He's becoming so, yes. My attack has…apparently changed things for him." She edged closer to him. Their fingers brushed. "He's feeling protective, he says. Clingy, I say."

"He cares about you." That knowledge shouldn't have made him angry, but it did.

"He likes conquests. I've seen it before. For some reason, he's decided that he needs *me* now. He was saying that he didn't even realize how he felt, not until he'd heard that I'd been taken."

Josh didn't move. "And how do you feel?"

Her head tipped back. "I feel like I'm staring at the man I want."

He wanted to kiss her. Right there, in that god-forsaken place. But…

Hold the thought. Do the search. Get her to safety.

He turned away. Shined the light at the stairs and then—

He swung right back toward her. His hand slid under her chin, he tipped her head back a bit more and he kissed her. Deep, quick, hard.

Enough to savor. Enough to tease.

"Josh?"

He stared into her eyes. "Just so you know, I'm staring at the woman I want." She didn't play games. He wouldn't, either. Then, taking her hand, they went up the stairs. He made sure to go first, a habit from the FBI and his SEAL days. If there was any threat there, he'd be facing it first.

At the top of the stairs, he turned into the first room on the left—it was the most finished room. The others still sported barely framed walls.

The room on the left—that had been the room she'd been held inside. The rope was gone. Sawdust was still on the ground, mixed with discarded pieces of wood.

Plastic had been put over one of the window spaces, but it flapped in the wind.

Casey slid past him. Her hand broke from his. "I woke up right there." She pointed to the floor. "He had to be strong, huh? To carry me up the stairs while I was out cold." She shivered. "He could have done anything to me then, and I wouldn't have known. I—" She shook her head. Straightened her shoulders. "I woke up right there," she said again, her voice stronger. "And I was alone in here. I screamed for help…"

But no help had come. Only the perp had come to her.

"I can smell the ocean," she whispered. Her eyes closed. "When he came in... I—I don't think I smelled the oil any longer. That means—he cleaned up, right? He must have cleaned up somewhere and then he came to me. He had his knife. He had the phone. He called the sheriff and—" Casey shook her head. "I'm not getting anything new. It's not working this time."

He wanted to pull her into his arms. But she was pacing, her movements tight and worried, and he held himself still.

She headed toward the window—not the one that overlooked the ocean, but the one that focused back toward the city. She stared out. "He must've had a car stashed somewhere, right? I mean, for him to get away so quickly. After I stabbed him, he hit me again." Her hand rose to feather over her cheek. "I fell back for a minute and he ran out. I was afraid to follow him at first. Afraid to move at all, and that was time that I wasted. Time that let him get away." She looked back at him. "So I know that if he does kill someone else, that's on me. I should have chased him. I should have stopped him. I—"

Josh had gone to her, helpless to stop himself. His hands closed around her shoulders. "You should have survived. That's the only thing you needed to do." He turned her to face him fully. "You fought him off. You gave Hayden your location. The perp probably did have a ride stashed somewhere nearby—

and he knows the area. He was able to vanish fast because—"

But his words stopped. He'd just...seen someone below. Hadn't he? It had been a quick flash of movement. Like a shadow rushing away from—his bike?

"Josh?"

He eased her to the side even as he pulled out his weapon. His gaze had narrowed as he fought to search through the growing darkness below. Yes, *yes*, someone was there. And—

He heard another motorcycle growl.

That was how he'd gotten away so fast. Since coming to Hope, Josh had realized there were quite a few people in the town who liked to use motorcycles and scooters—the smaller vehicles enabled them to access all of the trails that were scattered around Hope.

"He came back, too," Josh muttered. Because the perp had left something behind? Or because he just couldn't stay away from the scene of his kills? Josh whirled away from the window. "He's down there." And he was getting away.

No, that couldn't happen. Josh and Casey raced down the stairs. He shoved past that wooden front door and erupted into the darkness. He kept one hand wrapped around Casey's wrist and his other had his gun.

"I thought it was you," Casey said, her words tumbling out. "I heard the motorcycle that morning—but you were rushing into the cabin when I came down the stairs. That noise—*I thought it was you.*"

The perp had been clever. He'd used the sound of Josh's bike to mask his own departure.

Josh jumped onto his motorcycle and holstered his weapon. Casey grabbed her helmet, then she was holding him tight. He kicked up the stand and had the engine roaring to life. He took off, spraying up sand in his wake. He could see the other motorcycle up ahead. The driver was wearing a dark helmet, completely shielding his head. The driver was driving fast as hell as he turned on a sharp curve that led away from the beach.

"Hold on," Josh snapped. He braked a bit, trying to slow before the curve—

Something is wrong. The bike slowed, just a bit, but the control was off. There was a long, loud grinding noise that came from the motorcycle. *What in the hell?*

"Casey—"

The other driver had stopped. In the next moment, the fellow turned his motorcycle around, revved his engine and then took off, heading straight for Josh and Casey.

"Is he playing chicken?" she yelled. *"What is he doing?"*

He was coming right at them, and Josh's bike was out of control. He couldn't brake, and he smelled the bitter odor of oil.

Casey smelled oil in her hotel room.

The guy was almost on them. "Casey, you'll need to jump."

"What?"

He tried to steer toward the side of the road, but the motorcycle just gave another horrible groan of metal. The other driver was closing in. The SOB slammed the front of his motorcycle into Josh's bike. Josh and Casey went swerving. Their motorcycle hurtled across the road as sparks flew from the tires and spokes.

They were crashing, hitting too hard. Josh spun back and grabbed Casey, trying to get her off that bike and to safety.

But then he wrecked. The motorcycle didn't hit the soft sand dune he'd been aiming for, but it slammed into the hard base of a tree. The metal didn't just groan then. It screamed as both he and Casey went flying.

Chapter Twelve

She hurt. Casey moaned as she opened her eyes. She was on the ground and her whole body ached. When she lifted her hands, she felt the blood on her palms. When they'd crashed, she'd gone flying. She'd hit the pavement, hard, and the skin had torn off her hands—and maybe her knees. Her jeans were wet near her knees and she was—

Someone was standing over her. A man in a black motorcycle helmet. She still had her helmet on, too. "Josh?" Casey whispered. Had he been wearing a dark helmet? Was he—

The man lifted his gloved hand and she saw the knife he gripped tightly.

"Get away from her!" Josh's roar seemed to echo around her. *"Now! I'm a federal agent, and I am telling you to back away!"*

Casey kicked out with her feet, aiming for the guy's shin. He staggered and yelled behind the lowered visor of his helmet. She saw nothing in that darkness—nothing that told her who he was.

"Drop the knife!" Josh yelled.

The guy in the helmet lunged toward her as he swiped down with the knife.

Josh fired. The boom of the gun seemed to erupt around her. Her attacker staggered and the knife dropped from his hand. Josh had hit him high in the shoulder.

Casey shoved to her feet and stumbled back a few desperate steps. She could see Josh running toward her and the perp. Josh's gun was still out and aimed at her attacker. The guy had grabbed his shoulder. He whirled toward her.

Again, she saw only blackness.

But…she heard the rumble of another motor. One that was coming toward them. So fast.

She looked to the left and saw another motorcycle hurtling down the little road.

And—

The bike braked. The rider lifted his hand and Casey saw that he was armed, as well. Only not with a knife. A gun.

There are two of them.

"Get down, Casey!" Josh yelled.

She was already diving for cover. In the next instant, he was above her and she heard the blast of gunfire once more. Josh rolled them, tumbling them down the small sand dune, and she knew he was trying to shield them both.

Gunfire thundered once more, but nothing had

hit her. Her breath sawed from her lungs. *Safe*. For the moment and—

A motorcycle revved. Tires squealed.

"He's getting away," Josh snarled. "Stay down!" He leapt to his feet. She peeked up just enough to see him take aim and fire.

But it was too late.

Her attacker and the second rider—they were both gone.

"Damn it!" She could feel his fury, but in the next instant, Josh turned toward her and his voice shook with worry. "Casey! Are you hurt?"

"No, I'm okay." Scrapes, bruises, a little blood. Nothing fatal. She took off the helmet—she'd still been wearing the thing.

"My bike is trashed—I can't follow them." He'd yanked out his phone. "We need an APB out for them right now. *Two* of them. A team, I should have considered it… Two would make everything so much easier. Subduing the victims, transporting them. One could be lookout. One could drive the boat. The other could get rid of the body—"

She could still hear the roar of that motorcycle.

Josh had his phone to his ear. "Tucker, Tucker, listen man. I need you to start a hunt for two motorcycles. Yes, yes, listen to me. We were at the beach house and we were attacked. They just left us—get deputies and agents on the road *now*… Here's the description of the bikes…"

THEY FOUND THE MOTORCYCLES. They were located less than twenty minutes later. The bikes were dumped near the public beach. The place was deserted after sunset, and the perps had used that to their advantage.

Josh paced near the scene, fury riding him hard. "I let them get away."

Tucker sighed. "From the sound of things, you and Casey are both lucky to be alive." He shook his head. "You really think the guy tampered with your bike?"

"I know he did. The brakes were barely working, steering was a nightmare and we were freaking sitting ducks when he turned on us." The guy had set a trap and Josh had fallen right into it—and he'd nearly taken Casey down with him. "He was going to kill her. The bike was still on top of me, and I couldn't get to her fast enough."

Casey had been thrown, and thankfully she'd had the helmet on.

"She didn't like motorcycles," Josh muttered, raking a hand through his hair. "The first time I tried to get her on one..." His gaze sought her out. She was in the back of a patrol car—the sheriff's car—sitting still in the middle of that madness. "She didn't want to go with me. I had to convince her."

That moment seemed like it had occurred so long ago.

"You shot him?" Tucker prompted.

"In the right shoulder. So if you want to know

with certainty whether or not Kurt Anderson is our perp, you don't have to wait for tomorrow and the results of the blood work." His lips twisted. "Go find him right now. See if he has a gunshot wound."

Tucker nodded. "I already got agents searching for him right now."

They needed to search faster. "*Two* of them. Can't believe that—when the second rider came up, I barely had time to cover Casey."

"She's okay." Tucker gripped his shoulder. "She's safe."

"He came after her. *They* came after her. Just like we feared. She's in their sights, and they won't stop, not until they have her." He gave a grim shake of his head. "I'm not going to let that happen. Casey isn't going to wind up in the ocean. I won't go diving down there and find her that way—I can't." He forced his gaze to move away from her. His eyes met Tucker's. "She matters too much."

"Like that, is it?"

Too fast, too soon, but... Why deny it any longer? Why pretend? "Yes, it's like that."

Hayden came rushing up toward them. "The motorcycles were both reported stolen in Pensacola— that was four weeks ago."

Josh scraped his hand across the stubble on his cheek. "There's no way they transported the victims on those bikes. They used something else. Something that was at the scene of each crime. There must be a van or an SUV that they have—probably had it waiting right here at the beach so that they could make a clean getaway." But he didn't think they'd gone far. No, not far at all.

They would be hunting for Casey again soon.

The local authorities had fanned out, searching the scene. They were going up and down the beach, shining their flashlights across the sand as they searched for possible tracks or evidence.

"You should get Casey out of here," Tucker continued. "If we find something, I'll let you know. Screw what FBI brass said—she's obviously still a target, and her protection should be the FBI's priority."

Her protection was his priority. "I almost lost her." Josh shook his head. "It can't happen again." *It won't happen.* He stalked toward the sheriff's car.

"STAY STILL! THE bullet went right through you. I just need to stop the blood."

He clenched his back teeth against the pain. His body had been marked—for a second time. Not part of his plan. He liked to give the pain. Like to watch his victims moan and beg.

"I'm not supposed to be the one bleeding," he rasped.

The needle jabbed into his skin. A stitch job, to stop the blood. He'd carry that stupid mark forever now.

"Then maybe you shouldn't have gone off the

script and gone after them! I *told* you to wait. I told you I had things covered."

"I got sick of waiting." He was also sick of being told what to do. It had been his plan. His moves. His victims. "It's ending." He knew just how it would end, too. He'd known from the beginning.

"Yes, well, it's not over yet. While you were out screwing things to hell and back, I was eliminating loose ends. That guy at the dock? Chaz? I couldn't risk him talking. It was only going to be a matter of time."

The needle jabbed him again. He grunted. "He never saw me."

"No, he saw *me*. And I'm not going down for this." The needle stilled. "Do you understand me? We are in this together. You aren't going to leave me taking the fall."

Of course, I am. "Of course, not. You know we have a deal. I'll get what I want…and you'll get what you want. Everything will work out."

"Provided that Josh Duvane doesn't kill you first."

He laughed, but the sound held no humor. "I won't be the one dying."

The needle jabbed him once more. "Don't be so sure of that…"

And there was just something in that low tone… His eyes narrowed.

"But the first thing we have to do…we need to make sure the Feds have the right suspect in their sights."

JOSH WAS COMING toward her. Casey hurriedly climbed out of the patrol car. "Tell me you found something," she began.

"Agents! Sheriff Black!" a voice thundered out.

She whirled around and saw that Finn was running toward them. His flashlight bobbed. "Found… something…got to see…" He gasped out each word. "Body…" He motioned behind him. "On the beach… come on…"

They all rushed to follow him. The sand flew in their wake and sure enough…

Oh, God. She saw the body, sprawled on the shore. The waves were hitting it again and again. A man's body, facedown, a heavy gash near his forehead. The flashlights lit him up and she saw his swollen, too pale skin. She also saw the tribal tattoo around his upper arm—an arm that was cast out to his side.

"I know him." She wanted to look away, but couldn't.

"Chaz Fontel." Josh's voice was grim. "Damn it."

Yes, it was Chaz. He'd been talking to her— flirting with her—just hours before.

Now he was dead?

She looked up at Josh. He was still staring at the body, a hard frown on his face.

The wind blew against them, and the waves rushed toward their feet.

"I'M SORRY."

Casey's feet were dragging as she crossed the

threshold into the penthouse, but at Josh's words, she glanced back. "For what?"

He shut the door. Secured the lock. "For not taking better care of you."

"It's hardly your fault *two* psychos came after us tonight."

"I shouldn't have taken you to the beach house. The guy was obviously waiting there. I led you right into his trap."

She ignored the aches and pains in her body. "We were *both* in his trap. And I'm very glad that we're both okay right now."

He stared into her eyes. "I don't like for you to be hurt."

Casey offered him a wan smile. "Fair enough, I don't like being hurt, either." But her smile slipped away. The tension between them was so thick and dark. "Have you seen this before? Two killers, working together?"

"It's rare, but it happens. Tucker would say that one's usually the dominant and the other is following orders."

Right. "Do you think… Chaz's death has to be related, doesn't it? I mean, you saw his head—he'd been hit. More than a few times." She'd never get that image out of her mind. "He's talking to you— to me—and later the same day, he's dead. No way that's coincidence. He knew something, and someone out there didn't want him talking to us anymore."

His head inclined. "Looks that way."

Frustration beat at her. "Don't do that."

His brows lifted.

"Don't treat me like I'm just some reporter who is pressuring you for details on a case." She marched toward him and jabbed her index finger at his chest. "This is me. This is you. What's happening—it's about *us*. So don't pull rank and shut me out. You don't want me hurt? Fine, but understand this, I don't want *you* hurt, either. You matter, and because of me, you're in the crosshairs, too." Her words were fast and angry and she couldn't stop them. "You can't pull back on me now, so don't even think of doing it, got me? We're in this together. You and me, until the end." She sucked in a deep breath. "If that's a problem for you—"

He kissed her. The deep, toe-curling kind of kiss that she wanted. The kind that told her she was safe, that she was alive, and that the need between them was as strong as ever.

Fear wasn't going to stop her. Fear wasn't going to stop him.

This is you. This is me. This is us.

His hands were around her, warm and tight. Hers had locked around his shoulders. His head lifted and he stared into her eyes. "I was afraid I couldn't stop him."

"I was afraid you'd died when the motorcycle crashed." She'd flown through the air, helpless, and when she'd looked up... "How about we promise not to scare each other that way again?"

He nodded. His expression was still so tense.

He caught her hands and pulled them down. His gaze fixed on the bandages that covered her palms. "Just scratches," she said. "I must have...tried to brace myself when I hit the pavement."

"You were lucky."

They both had been. "Luck won't last forever."

"We'll catch them."

She had to believe that.

"You want to shower?" Josh asked her. "It will make you feel better. Wash away the bruises and the aches."

Sounded like a plan to her. "Come with me?"

He smiled. The smile didn't lighten his eyes. "You get the water going and I'll be right behind you."

She turned away from him and headed for the hallway, but she hesitated and had to glance back. Casey found him staring after her with a hard, hooded gaze. She faltered. "Josh?"

"I will do *anything* to keep you safe." His eyes glittered. "I hope you know that."

She did. Once, a man had tried to destroy her by taking away all that she held dear. Josh was the opposite of Benjamin. She saw that so clearly. He was a protector. Fierce and dangerous, yes, but at his heart, he was a man who would fight desperately for the victims.

He'd fight desperately for her.

Did he know...she'd fight just as desperately for him?

KURT ANDERSON STARED at the prison. His old man was in there, locked away behind the heavy walls and secured behind the bars. He wanted his father to rot. To *never* get out. To never be free.

It was exactly what the guy deserved.

Kurt lifted the beer to his mouth, but stopped, catching himself. Sarah had told him not to drink again. She said that when he drank, he didn't think clearly. He made mistakes. He wasn't supposed to make mistakes anymore.

Why am I even out here? He should be at home, but…at his house, the reporters kept showing up. He'd told them to stay off his property, but they were still there.

Only this time…they were asking him different questions. Asking him if *he* was the killer.

He wasn't. He'd *never* be like his father.

He shifted his car into Park. He needed to get out of there before some of the guards came toward him. They'd ask questions. Hell, they might even call Sheriff Black. The last thing he wanted was to deal with that guy again. Did Hayden think he didn't see the hate in his eyes? Every time that Hayden looked at him, Kurt knew it was there. Hayden blamed him for what had happened to Jillian West. Hayden had *always* been crazy for Jill, and Kurt's dad had nearly destroyed her.

He blames me. Just as much as he blames my father.

What Hayden didn't get—what no one in that

town seemed to get—was that Kurt blamed himself, too. He should have stopped his father. He should have seen the truth, so long ago.

He backed out of the lot, sending gravel spitting up from his tires. He wasn't going back home. He'd find some little motel and crash for the night. Maybe tomorrow, he'd listen to Sarah and start the therapy that she kept trying to shove down his throat. It was just that he'd thought that sharing crap wasn't for him.

But I can't keep going on this way. Hayden actually thought I might be a killer.

He wouldn't be. He *couldn't* be.

His phone rang, startling him. It was his personal line. He'd only given that number out to a few people.

He braked on the side of the road and, fumbling, he pulled out his phone. He stared at the number and name on his screen, confused. *Casey Quinn.* Right. He'd given her his number after their last meeting. When he'd thought she might actually tell his side of things.

Before she'd been taken.

Why in the hell was she calling him?

Curious, he swiped his thumb over the screen. "This is Kurt."

"I need your help..."

Chapter Thirteen

She'd taken off her bandages. Stripped. Slid beneath the warm spray of the shower. Casey had left the lights on. She could have showered in the dark. Could have hidden in the dark. But she didn't want to do that.

She was tired of hiding.

For years, she felt as if she'd just been pretending to be someone else. Cassidy had become Casey and she'd bottled up all of her fears. She'd locked herself down, not letting anyone close. She'd reported on other victims in an attempt to help them.

But inside, she'd stayed the same frightened girl.

She put her head under the spray, and maybe she used it to wash away the tears that trickled down her face. There was so much pain out there—the world was full of pain. But if you really looked, it was also full of good things, too.

She heard the squeak of the door opening. Her head lifted and she saw Josh standing in the doorway. With his eyes on her, he stripped. There was no hesitation from him. No shyness. She wasn't entirely sure he understood the concept of shyness. Not Josh.

He eased open the glass door and slid into the shower with her. It was a truly massive space, easily big enough for them both. He grabbed the soap and then his big, rough hands were gently washing her skin. Massaging her as he tried to take away her aches and pains.

She closed her eyes and turned her face back toward the spray.

Then she felt his hand still on her back, right over the old scar that had marked her for so long. The scar that had changed her life—and her—forever.

There was a light, soft feathering over the scar and she glanced back—he was kissing the scar. Using such tenderness with her. Her heart ached as she turned to lock her arms around him. Their bodies were wet and steam drifted in the air around them. Their lips met. The kiss was slow at first, sensual as his tongue stroked past her lips. Her breasts pressed to his body, her nipples tight and aching. Every time they came together, the need surprised her. The way the desire built and twisted within her, a hunger that wasn't weakening. It was just growing stronger the more that she was with him.

He reached behind her and turned off the water. The last *drip, drip, drip* seemed too loud. They didn't speak as they slipped from the shower. Right then, Casey didn't think there needed to be any words. He took a towel and dried her carefully, being extra gentle near her palms and her bruised knees. Then it was her turn. She picked up a towel and slid it over his chest. Her mouth followed the towel's path. Kissing. Savoring. She pressed her lips to every inch of him.

His body shuddered beneath her touch. She was pretty sure her own desire was making her tremble. She took his hand and led him back into the bedroom. In moments, he had on protection and he was sliding into her. He filled her completely, so perfectly. Her breath came faster, her heart raced and the gentle pace gave way to fierce need. Her nails raked over his back. Her hips surged up to meet him. He slid in and out of her, and Casey had to bite her lip to muffle her cries.

"Don't." He stilled. "Give me everything. That's what I'll give you."

He withdrew, only to thrust deep. Her legs locked around his hips and Casey let go. She cried out as the pleasure hit her, and he was right with her, driving hard until he found his own release. Then he shouted her name.

No holding back, not for either of them.

Not ever again.

HER PHONE WAS ringing again. Casey opened her eyes. She was still in bed, but Josh wasn't there. Her hand slid out but the pillow next to her was cool to the touch, as if Josh had been gone awhile.

Her phone rang again.

She frowned even as she rose from the bed. It

took a few stumbling moments, but Casey found the phone discarded on the floor. Her finger swiped across the screen. "Hello?"

"Kurt Anderson is missing!" Tom said, his voice sharp. "He's missing and I just saw about your attack on the *news*. On a freaking competing show! What in the actual *hell*, Casey?"

She blinked and tried to push her sleepiness away. It was still early, barely 10:00 p.m. according to the clock on the bedside table. She'd just crashed hard after making love with Josh.

Where is he? She wrapped a sheet around herself, toga-style, and crept toward the bedroom door. The door squeaked when she pulled it open. "I'm sorry—I didn't think to stop and call you while the guy was shooting at me."

"*Casey.* I care about you—this isn't about the story! This is about my *friend* getting hurt. I'm worried! We've known you for years." His voice actually shook. "I want to know you're okay. Are you still with the agent? Is he keeping you safe?"

She'd reached the den. "I'm at the safe house."

"Casey..." He sighed. "Did you hear what I said about Kurt Anderson? He's *missing*. You're attacked and the guy goes missing. He's coming for you. I know it."

"He'll have a hard time getting to me." Not with the security at that place.

Josh stepped from the kitchen. He was completely dressed—dressed in his khaki pants and button-up shirt. His "FBI clothes" as she thought of them. And he had his holster in place. He frowned when he saw her.

"I can send your bodyguards over," Tom said quickly. "Katrina said they were down at the club having a drink, and she just went to get them. They'll be back in no time. Let me send them to you. Let me help—"

"I'm all right for now. I just— Let me talk to Josh for a moment, okay? I'll call you back, I promise." Because she had to ask him about Kurt. Had to ask why it looked as if he were about to walk right out of that place without her. She ended the call and set the phone on the counter. "Josh, that was Tom. He said Kurt Anderson is missing."

A muscle jerked in Josh's jaw. "The Feds couldn't find him at his house or any of his usual hangouts. The cops tried tracking his phone, but turned up nothing. His lawyer says he's just gone to cool off but..."

"But you don't buy it."

"He could be on the water," Josh said. "At least, that's what Hayden thinks. When it was cut-and-run time for his father, Theodore Anderson tried to go out on a blaze of glory on the water. With the victims turning up in the ocean, it seems like that might be a possibility we can't ignore."

"Do they want you on the search?"

He shook his head. "I'm not leaving you." His jaw hardened. "And...there's no reason for me to dive into the water. We aren't looking for a victim—we don't have one yet—"

Her phone rang. She glanced at the screen and recognized the number there. *Katrina.*

"Go ahead," Josh said. "Let your friends know that you're all right."

She exhaled and grabbed the phone. Casey answered and quickly said, "Katrina, listen, I don't need the guards right now. Josh is with me and—"

"I've got someone new," a low voice rasped.

She almost dropped the phone.

"It's time for you to find her."

Casey lunged forward and grabbed Josh's arm. Then she frantically switched the phone to the speaker option so that he could hear—

"She's going to die in your place. Hardly fair, isn't it? I mean, she doesn't even have any secrets to tell me. She isn't like the others. There's no story with her."

"Who is this?" Casey demanded.

He laughed. "I have your friend. And she's going to start bleeding soon. Too bad you got away. I never would have gone after her. But you made me so mad tonight. I don't like getting shot, you see. Now someone else has to feel the pain."

"Don't!" Casey cried out. "You don't have to hurt her."

"Don't have to do anything," that low rasp told her. "Want to do it."

Josh had his own phone out. He was texting rapidly and she knew he was probably messaging Tucker and Hayden.

"Think you can find her?" the caller taunted her. "Sheriff Black never got to them in time. Do you really think you can?"

Her frantic gaze met Josh's. She didn't know where the perp was—she had no clue. The last time she'd seen him, he'd been rushing away on that motorcycle.

"The agent is with you, isn't he? Josh Duvane. He finds my bodies. He brings them to the surface. Duvane…do you think you can find me?" Laughter drifted to them. "But then, you've already been looking, haven't you? Looking, but not finding. I've been right there, and you couldn't catch me."

"I could shoot you, though," Josh growled. "I'm the one who did that. Not Casey. Not Katrina. So if you want to hurt someone, why don't you try me? Or do you just enjoy targeting the people who you think are weaker than you? What kind of man gets off on torturing women, anyway?"

Silence.

Casey's eyes had widened. She knew Josh was deliberately taunting the guy. Trying to pull his focus so that the perp would take out his rage on Josh.

"You think you can face me?" The caller's rasp was even rougher. "Come on, try, FBI Agent. Come face me. You take me down and the woman can go."

Where was he?

"I'm up high," the guy continued. "I can see for

miles. My light is shining. I'll see you coming. If you bring someone else with you, if you bring backup, I'll know. Just you and me, Agent Duvane. You come alone, you face me and maybe I'll let both of the women go. Or maybe...maybe you'll be the one who dies."

Casey shook her head. She mouthed *no*, but Josh said, "The lighthouse. That's where you are, right, you SOB? Up high, with your light shining...you're at the old lighthouse out near the jetties. The place was supposed to be condemned."

The caller laughed. "I think I'll get started. Katrina has some secrets to share."

A woman screamed.

The call ended.

Goose bumps had risen on Casey's arms. "No. You can't go in alone."

He was checking his weapon.

She wanted to shake him. "He'll kill you. *They'll* kill you. We know he has a partner. He could just be waiting to shoot you on sight. Then he'll kill you and Katrina." Her voice was rising. "You can't follow his orders!"

He gave her a grim smile. "You really think I'd play by his rules?"

She hoped to God not.

"Tucker and I will handle him. He'll never see Tucker coming. Hayden Black will have our backs—that guy knows how to go in undetected. I'm not fool enough to go in that place alone, not knowing there are *two* of them out there. He has a partner, so I'll have two partners." He nodded grimly. "This is ending tonight. He *wants* a final face-off. That's why he's calling. The guy is breaking apart, and I'm going to be there when he shatters into a million pieces."

That didn't sound good.

"You stay here," Josh told her gruffly. "This place is secure. You're safe. The building has a security guard stationed below *and* Hayden sent Finn over to stand watch downstairs a bit earlier. I'll get him to come up here."

"I don't need guarding. You do. Katrina does. Don't worry about me!"

But he stared into her eyes. "I'll always worry about you." His hand rose and touched her cheek. "I've still got my laptop set to receive the security feeds from the building. You can see everything that's happening outside this penthouse."

"I'll be fine."

A muscle jerked in his jaw. "I'll be back before you know it."

She locked her hand tightly around his. "Be careful. You'd better not have so much as a single new scratch on you when you get back."

His slow smile flashed. "Sweetheart, you keep talking like that, and I'll think you care."

She didn't smile back. "I do care, Josh. I care a whole lot…because I think I'm falling for you."

Shock flashed on his face.

"So come back to me. Come back safe." She kissed him. *Come back safe.*

JOSH RUSHED FROM the elevator, his phone at his ear. "Yes, yes, Tucker, we're closing in on him. I'll be there in ten minutes." He hung up and waved to the deputy who'd been stationed in the lobby. "Finn, Casey is still upstairs. Go up there and make sure she stays secure, got it? Keep watch up there and don't let anyone else in the penthouse."

Finn nodded. "Got it."

Casey's words rang through Josh's mind as he hurried out toward the SUV that waited. Good thing he had a backup rental vehicle, especially considering that his motorcycle had been totaled. *I care a whole lot...because I think I'm falling for you.*

He jumped into the vehicle, cranked the engine and shoved the gear into Reverse. He wanted this threat to Casey eliminated. He wanted to find Katrina alive. This time, things were going to be different.

This time, the victim had a chance. And he was going to fight with every bit of his power to make sure that the perps out there—the two sadistic perps who'd killed three women in that town—were stopped.

FINN ROLLED BACK his shoulders as he rode the elevator up to the penthouse. He wouldn't screw this up.

Casey's safety would come first to him. He'd prove that he was good at his job. No more screwups.

The elevator opened.

A man stood near the door to the penthouse, bent over the lock. *What in the hell?*

Finn's hand immediately went to his holster, but the guy was whirling around, alerted by the ding of the elevator doors.

Light glinted off the man's glasses and his face flashed with relief when he saw Finn. "Thank goodness you're here, Deputy! I heard Casey scream."

What? Finn recognized Casey's producer, Tom.

"She called me—said Agent Duvane had to leave and for me to come over right away."

Finn had been downstairs, checking the guests who came back to the condominium with the security guard who'd been stationed there. He didn't remember seeing Tom come through the check-in. And Josh had *just* left…

"I got here—I heard her scream." Tom's eyes were bulging behind the glasses. "I think she's hurt in there—I think…I think that freak has her! He lured Josh away and now he has Casey." He pounded on the door. "We have to get to her! She's in trouble! Do you have a key?"

Finn's fingers still hovered over his gun.

"She needs help, damn it! We have to help her!"

He hesitated. Josh had *just* left. How had Tom gotten up to the penthouse so quickly?

CASEY HURRIED OUT of the bedroom. After Josh had left, she'd gone to dress as quickly as she could. There was no way she'd just hang around in a sheet while she waited to find out what was going to happen next. He'd taken her phone with him, just in case the perp called again, and she felt lost as she rushed back into the den and checked the security feed.

Finn. Tom.

Her lips parted. They were both right outside the front door. Had Finn brought Tom up? How had Tom gotten there so quickly? She turned for the door even as she heard someone pound against the wood. "I'm coming!" Casey yelled. She hurried forward. Her fingers curled around the lock. She fumbled, opening it quickly. She yanked the door open. "Tom!" Her breath heaved out as both men whirled toward her. "The killer has Katrina! But Josh is going to get her—she'll be okay." *I hope. I hope she's okay. She has to be okay.*

He nodded. "I—I know." He smiled at her. There was something about that smile…

How did he know?

Tom's hand whipped up—only it didn't come at her. He drove his hand right toward Finn's chest. His hand—and the knife that he'd gripped in his fist. The blade sank into Finn's body and a choked gasp broke from the deputy.

"Finn!" Casey slammed into Tom, knocking him back. Finn staggered, then his knees seemed

to give way as he fell to the floor, the knife still in his chest. *"Finn!"*

But Tom grabbed her from behind, yanking her up against him. "Don't worry, love. I've got another knife for you." And he pulled her back into the penthouse, slamming the door shut behind them.

Locking her inside…with him.

Chapter Fourteen

Josh pulled on his bulletproof vest. He and Tucker were in the shadows, well away from the lighthouse. The spotlight was on at that place, blazing out, circling into the water, but as far as he knew, the lighthouse should have been shut down.

"Who's been paying the power bill?" he muttered.

"Hayden checked on it—nothing is shut down here for another month." Tucker had his vest in place. His voice was guarded, and he seemed…oddly hesitant as he stood in the darkness. They were far enough away from the lighthouse that any watchers up there wouldn't see them, not yet. "It feels like another game."

"It *is* a game—one that has a woman's life as the prize."

Hayden slipped from the darkness and closed in on them. "I scouted the area. There's one car near the lighthouse." His voice was a gruff rumble. "I know that car—it belongs to Kurt Anderson."

Hell.

"You go in first," Tucker said to Josh even as he checked his own weapon. "I'll be right behind you."

"I'll have lookout," Hayden added. "I've got my night-vision gear ready. We'll be ahead of every move these guys make."

Josh hoped so. He stuck to cover as much as he could, moving quickly toward the lighthouse. When he neared the car—Kurt's car—he paused a moment and put his hand on the hood.

Cold. The guy had been there awhile.

Josh slipped inside—the front door was partially ajar. The place smelled old, stale. His eyes quickly adjusted to the darkness, a good thing because he didn't want to risk shining a light in there and giving his location away. He looked up, noting the spiral staircase and the illuminated peak of the lighthouse. The only light in the whole building came from that spotlight, but it was shining out, not down, so he stayed in the dark. There was a room to his right—probably the old office in the place. He edged closer to it. The door was shut.

He pushed it open and went in fast, coming up in a crouch.

A new scent hit him. Coppery. Acrid.

Blood.

There was no furniture in that room, nothing at all but the body. He could see the man lying in the middle of the room. He looked more like a twisted heap than a person.

"I'm FBI Agent Josh Duvane!" He called out, just in case this was some kind of trick. "Identify yourself!"

But the heap didn't move.

Josh rushed forward. There was a gun on the floor near the downed man, inches from his hand. Josh kicked that weapon away. He kept his own gun in his right hand even as he reached for the other man's shoulder.

Blood. Soaking wet with blood...because there was a gunshot wound to the guy's shoulder.

In the exact same spot Josh had shot the perp who'd come at him and Casey. He pulled out his light and shined it at the man's face.

Kurt Anderson's skin was a stark white. Blood trickled from his pale lips, and his eyes were closed. Josh swore as he lowered the light over the rest of the man's body. There was another gunshot wound to the fellow's stomach. And so much blood.

"Josh!"

Tucker ran in after him. Josh glanced up. "It's Anderson." His hand went to the man's throat. The guy's skin was cold but...was that a pulse? Faint? Thready? He pushed harder, searching for that sign of life.

"The rest of the place is clear. Katrina isn't here." Tucker dropped to his knees beside Josh. He gave a low whistle. "This isn't right. This whole scene... *it's wrong.*"

Wrong because their victim was missing. Wrong because—

Kurt's pulse jumped beneath Josh's fingers. "He's alive."

Tucker immediately started applying pressure to the man's stomach wound.

"Not…me…" Kurt whispered, the words little more than pained gurgle. "Not…"

Josh's shoulders stiffened. *It was a game, all right. All along.* A setup. He'd been lured to the lighthouse, but the victim wasn't there…

Because Katrina was never the victim that the perp really wanted.

Casey…she was the victim he'd wanted. And she was the woman who Josh had left behind.

HE'D HANDCUFFED HER.

Casey sat at the kitchen table, her hands cuffed behind her back, and she stared up at Tom—a Tom she didn't know, not at all.

He'd pulled out another knife from his boot—and he'd put that knife to her throat as he stared into her eyes.

"Why are you doing this?"

He shrugged, rolling his shoulders, then stopped to wince.

Because he's hurt! Now she realized that his right shoulder appeared a little bigger than the left, as if… he had bandages beneath his shirt.

"Casey…" He sighed out her name. "You're my star reporter. In your last moments on earth, I really expected you to have better questions. *Why are you doing this?* I mean, that's just so typical. I wanted more from you."

"And I wanted my producer *not* to be a killer!" The words shot from her.

He smiled. "There we go. Got a little fight back, huh?"

She blinked. "You aren't going to get away with this—"

"And we're back to boring."

"Josh will figure out it's you! There's a dead body in the hallway. There is no way he will think—"

Tom leaned in close to her. "I have a secret." He smiled. "You thought you were the only one with a secret?" The knife cut into her throat. "So wrong. I have a big one. That secret will be here soon."

Her heart felt as if it were about to rip right out of her chest.

He backed away from her. "We have to work fast, though, there isn't a lot of time."

Then he started opening drawers in the kitchen, one right after the other. She jerked against the cuffs even as her eyes stayed on his gloved hands. The same gloves he'd worn before…

"Here we go." He lifted up a roll of duct tape. "Perfect." He ripped off a piece, came back to her and slapped it over her lips. "If you're not going to say anything useful, then you'd better not say anything at all."

Her nostrils flared. The cuffs bit into her wrists.

"I'm going to stab you. Actually, I'm going to stab

you a lot. You'll hurt. You'll bleed, and then your FBI agent will come back to find your body." He leaned in close to her once more. His lips feathered over her ear. "But don't worry—I'll have killed the sick animal who attacked you. I'll be the hero."

The hell he would—

There was a rap at the door.

Her gaze snapped to the side, desperate, as she tried to look toward that door.

He stalked away from her, holding the knife. She saw him head toward the laptop—and the security feed. "Ah...and here she is. Just in time." He tucked the knife behind his back. He disappeared from view.

Casey twisted her wrists, struggling desperately. The jerk had learned from last time. No more rope. She couldn't cut or twist her way out of the handcuffs. They were too strong. But he'd left her legs free, his mistake. So she shoved down hard with her feet and rocked back, sending the chair crashing to the floor. Part of the wooden back broke beneath her, and she squirmed, getting her arms from behind the remains of that chair. She rolled and pushed to her feet.

"Casey?" Katrina was suddenly in front of her, staring with wide, shocked eyes.

Tom was right behind her friend. He'd hidden the knife. He'd—

He didn't need to hide it.

Casey stilled.

Tom had said that he had a secret, a big one. And

the perp hadn't been working alone—she and Josh knew that truth. A woman had screamed on the line when the killer had called her. And Casey had been so sure she was hearing Katrina's scream.

Because I was.

"Sorry, Casey," Katrina said, her lips curving down. "But it's time for someone else to be the star. I'm done working behind the camera. This is it for me. My big break."

What?

"The cops are going to find the Sandy Shore Killer. I left him dead in the lighthouse, complete with a gunshot wound to the shoulder. They're going to find him, and I'll give them a terrible, sad story about how I had to fight my way to freedom. I'll have injuries, of course. A knife wound or two to prove the terrible hell I've been through. And I'll say that the killer's accomplice ran away when I got the gun from Kurt."

From Kurt? Kurt Anderson? They're trying to pin all of this on Kurt?

"I'll be the story. You'll be another dead victim. Sorry, but in this business, sometimes, you really have to be ready to do the dirty work if you want to hit the big time."

Dirty work? They were *killing*.

"Let's get rid of her first," Katrina said, nodding, as she glanced back at Tom. "And then I'll get a slash or two—"

He was already slashing.

Casey tried to scream as she lunged forward, but Tom had driven his knife into Katrina's chest.

"I think you need more than a slash," he said. He caught Katrina's body as she slumped. "For this story to work, the partner has to be dead."

Casey kept rushing forward. She plowed her body into Katrina's slumped form—and into Tom. They all fell to the floor, landing in a heap. Casey rolled away fast, then she brought her cuffed hands up beneath her now kneeling legs. She strained and maneuvered until her hands were in front of her, and then she ripped the duct tape off her mouth, barely feeling the sting. "You bastard!" she yelled. She grabbed for Katrina.

The knife was still in Katrina's chest. Her eyes were open, wide, shocked.

Blood was pumping from her, covering her shirt. Her lips parted, as if she'd speak.

Tom laughed. "Can you believe she truly thought she'd be my next lead reporter? She never had the killer instinct."

A soft gasp slid from Katrina's lips. Her eyes closed.

Casey's hand curled around the hilt of that knife.

"Did you know…if you take the knife out, she'll just bleed out faster? I read that once—somewhere. If you leave a knife inside the person, they actually have a better chance of survival. It's when you take it out—and all of that blood starts pumping so frantically from the body—that's when the victim dies."

"I think she's already dead." Casey was pretty sure he'd stabbed Katrina straight in the heart.

"Yes, you're right." And she heard a sound behind her, a long glide, almost a *whish* of air.

Casey glanced back. He'd pulled a butcher knife from the block on the counter.

"Got a new weapon," he said, still smiling. "So why don't we get this show moving?"

Casey yanked the knife from Katrina's body. The other woman didn't move at all. *She's gone.* Casey clutched the bloody weapon with her right hand—still wearing the handcuffs. She whirled on Tom. "Stay away from me."

"Can't do that. You have to die, you see. Just as Katrina had to die. She was useful, for a time. After all, I needed someone to rent the boat for me so I could dump the bodies—couldn't very well do the renting myself. That would have created a trail and just come back to bite me in the ass."

She thought of Chaz's bloated body, washing up on the shore.

"Katrina was worried the boat manager would tell the cops about her. He would have, of course, eventually. The guy obviously loved being the center of a story. It would have worked in with my plan perfectly, but she got nervous…and Katrina took matters into her own hands."

Katrina had killed Chaz?

"Right now, your lover is finding the body of Kurt Anderson. Kurt has been quite shot up, by the way. A bullet went in and out of his right shoulder. And another—well, it was a gut shot. Highly painful. A terrible way to die, or at least, that's what I've been told."

She backed away from the kitchen—from Katrina's prone body—and tried to ease toward the front door. He followed her, stepping right over Katrina as if she didn't matter at all.

"Eventually, Agent Duvane will make his way back here. He'll find the dead deputy in the hallway. He'll find you, stabbed in this den, and then he'll find me…grief stricken as I huddle over Katrina's body. I had to kill her, you see. I came here, I realized what she'd done—I realized she'd been working with the killer all along—and I had to stop her before anyone else died." He sighed dramatically. "I just wish I'd found you sooner. Maybe I could have saved you."

"You're sick."

"No, I'm smart. I'm a man who knows how to create a killer story. When the situation presented itself, I had to act." His jaw hardened. "It's all Kylie's fault."

Kylie? Kylie Shane? The first victim?

"She recognized me. Can you believe that? It's been *years*, but she knew it was me. Saw me on the beach while you were filming a segment. I looked up—and she was staring at me as if she'd seen a ghost."

Her lips felt numb as she said, "When she was sixteen, Kylie was attacked. Stabbed twice, by an unknown assailant."

His smile came again. "Not really unknown…but

I did get away. I wanted to see what it was like, you see. To drive a knife into a pretty girl."

Nausea rolled in her stomach. *He'd wanted to see years ago...and he was still stabbing women now.*

"I knew Kylie recognized me. I couldn't let her talk. She had to die." He took another step toward her.

Casey took a frantic step back. The front door was locked—could she get it unlocked before he was on her? Could she stab him before he stabbed her?

"But after Kylie was dead, well, I saw the interest buzzing in town. A new story. A better killer... So I found another victim, and I kept going. It's easy to spot the wounded, you see. You just have to know what to look for." He laughed. "Bridget still had a limp, courtesy of her hit-and-run. I met her at a club, asked her what had happened, and the woman just told me *everything*. I was a complete stranger. She should have been more careful."

It was hard to be careful with a killer.

"And Tonya? Her scars were out for the world to see. I knew she'd be perfect." His smile still curled his lips. "I knew about you, of course. I make a point of learning everyone's secrets." He glanced back at Katrina. "Like Kat over there? The woman has a bit of a drug problem. She'd do anything to get what she needed. *Anything*."

She was going to run for the door.

"You had been attacked before. I understood how fragile you were. Sometimes, I could see you almost breaking in front of the camera. I think that was what the viewers loved about you—you weren't perfect. You were weak, just like everyone is. Got to say, though, I never expected you to fight back."

Her hand was slick around the knife. "I don't believe in giving up easily."

"No?" His brows rose. "Thanks for the warning. Now, sorry, but we really need to hurry along. Can't have Agent Duvane arriving before you're dead."

He rushed toward her. She spun and grabbed for the door, fumbling with that lock. She managed to get the lock to turn, managed to rip the door open—

The blade sank into her shoulder. Casey cried out and her bound hands flew out as she whirled back to him—she stabbed at him, hitting his arm again and again with the blade. Hacking at him. He swore and jumped back.

She could feel the blood on her back. Sliding over her skin, soaking her shirt. She rushed through the doorway.

"Casey!"

Josh was there. He caught her in his arms and stared at her with wide, blazing eyes.

"He…he's in there… *Knife*…"

And she still had her knife, too. It was gripped in her hands.

Josh pushed her behind him. He had a gun in one hand, and Tucker Frost—Tucker was right there, too. His face was just as grim as Josh's.

She looked back at the doorway. She'd expected

Tom to follow her out. He hadn't. What was he doing in there? The penthouse seemed dead quiet.

And then…

Laughter.

The door was still open, just a few inches.

"You're back too soon…she's not dead," Tom called out.

Josh's hold on Casey's hand tightened.

"If you don't all leave, I'll kill her right now. I'll slit her throat, from ear to ear."

What? She wasn't even in there with him any longer. She was safe. She was—

Josh pushed open the door to the penthouse.

Katrina.

Tom stood in the middle of the den, and Katrina was slumped in his arms. He had his knife at her throat. Her head was tilted down, her lashes closed.

"I think she's already dead," Casey whispered.

"Is she?" Tom shouted. "Don't be so sure. Things aren't always what they seem." He jabbed the tip of the knife into Katrina's throat.

Katrina's body jerked.

Josh swore. Then he was shoving Casey farther back. "Sweetheart, get to the elevator. Go downstairs— get *out* of here—"

"Don't go anywhere, Casey! I'm not finished with you!" Tom bellowed.

She froze.

"Casey Quinn. Casey Too-Good-For-Me Quinn. But you weren't too good for the agent, were you?

The night I took you, I was watching when he brought you back to the hotel on his motorcycle. I saw the way you looked at him, the way you let him touch you. You played hands-off with me, but I saw the truth…and I knew you were going to feel my knife."

Tucker slipped into the penthouse. His gun was aimed at Tom. "It's over. Let the woman go, now."

"Nothing's over. It's just beginning. I'm beginning. And *you're* the one leaving. You and Agent Duvane are going to walk out of this building. If you don't, I'll slit Katrina's throat right here and now."

Casey knew he would.

"You'll walk away," Tom continued. "Casey will stay. And then I'll—"

"You'll kill them both," Josh said, his voice a hard growl. "That's not happening. You aren't going to touch Casey again."

She trembled, her shoulder throbbing and the blood soaking her.

Josh edged into the open doorway. He and Tucker fanned out a bit, closing in on Tom. Casey knew she should probably run, but…her legs trembled. *How much blood am I losing?* She grabbed on to the door frame so she wouldn't fall. Her hands were bloody. She'd gotten Katrina's blood on her when she grabbed the knife.

"Casey!" Tom shouted her name.

Her head whipped up. She stared straight at him.

"This isn't the ending I wanted."

She knew that. "You…you went to the prison. You're the one who kept trying to convince…Theodore Anderson…to talk to me…"

"I also convinced him that his son was an ungrateful failure who deserved to be punished. Theodore was all too eager to point the finger at Kurt. Everything would have been perfect." He sighed and his shoulders slumped a bit. "But they came back too soon." His gaze swept to Josh. "Couldn't stay away from her, huh? Have to be close, every moment. There was another man who fell for Casey that way. Fell so deep and hard that he killed for her."

"I never wanted Benjamin to kill," she whispered.

"You'll have to kill, too, Agent Duvane," Tom continued. Katrina seemed to be a dead weight in his arms. "Because I'm not stopping. Casey will see you kill. She'll know you're just like the other one. She'll turn from you. You'll lose her as surely as if I put my knife in her heart."

"No!" Casey yelled.

He looked at her. Smiled. "I chose the ending. It was my story, never yours." His hand tightened around that knife, and she knew, she *knew* he was going to slit Katrina's throat.

Casey screamed and raced forward.

Gunshots blasted.

One shot hit Tom in the shoulder. The other…in the head.

He fell back. The knife cut across Katrina's neck, but it didn't sink deep.

Tucker and Josh both closed in. Tucker kicked the knife away from Tom, and Josh grabbed for Katrina. Casey's breath heaved from her as she hurried to Josh's side. The shot to head—it had killed Tom. She'd seen—no, she didn't want to think about what she'd seen as that bullet tore into him.

Josh was pressing his hands to Katrina's wounds. Tucker was on his phone, demanding to know where backup was, and Casey—

"It was my shot," Josh said, not looking up as he worked frantically on Katrina. "My shot killed him. I did it."

"I know." Somehow, she'd just...known.

His head turned. "I'd do it again in a heartbeat. He wasn't going to hurt you again."

Her lips were trembling.

"I'd do it again," he said quietly.

A tear slid down her cheek.

I know.

KATRINA WELCH HADN'T SURVIVED. Josh stood in the condominium's parking lot, the swirl of police lights illuminating the scene. A gurney rushed past him— Finn was strapped down and two medics were working feverishly on him. The knife was still in his chest, and he was still breathing, barely. Josh hoped the kid survived.

There had been enough death.

"No, no, I don't want to leave!"

His head whipped to the right at the sound of *her*

voice. Casey was in the back of an ambulance. She should have been on the way to the hospital, but the woman was trying to push her way past the team surrounding her. She looked over at him. Their gazes locked. "Josh!"

Instantly, he ran toward her. She'd been stabbed—her blood had soaked her clothes. "She needs to get to a hospital right now," he snarled, glaring at the EMTs. "What are you waiting for—"

"You," Casey said.

He shook his head.

"I can't leave without you." She licked her lips. The EMTs pushed her back onto the gurney. "He was wrong. Tom was *crazy*. I don't see you differently. You're a good agent, Josh. A good man. I need you to know that."

His chest seemed to burn. He should stay at the scene, help Tucker tie up loose ends but...

Casey.

He climbed into the back of the ambulance. His hand caught hers. Did she get it? To him, Tom Warren had been a dead man the instant Josh saw the guy holding that bloody knife. Tom had come after Casey time and time again. Josh had never intended to let him walk.

Did she understand?

"I'm sorry—" his voice came out rough "—that you were hurt." He looked down at her wrist. The handcuffs were gone and dark bruises banded her wrists. "I should have kept you safe."

He'd nearly lost her.

"You can't save the world."

It wasn't the world that mattered to him right then. It was Casey. And when he'd raced back to the penthouse, so desperate to get to her, every instinct in his body screaming at him that something was wrong— to get *to* her…he'd felt something splinter inside of him. He'd tried calling the condominium's front desk, but the line had been disabled. Before he'd gone upstairs, Tom had been busy. He'd taken out the phone line and even turned off the alarm so that he could access the top floor via the service elevator. Since he'd gone through the service area, the guard in the lobby hadn't seen the fellow. Tom had been smart.

Sadistic.

Josh was glad he was dead.

When he couldn't reach Casey, Josh had tried calling Finn—no answer. He'd demanded backup at the condo building even before he'd rushed inside, but that backup hadn't arrived soon enough to help.

It had been him and Tucker.

"He chose death," Casey said. "That was on him. He did that. He could have dropped his knife. You were trying to save Katrina."

He stared into her eyes. Her beautiful, dark eyes. The woman had gotten to him. She'd gone far beneath his skin and straight into the soul that felt battered. "I didn't want to lose you." Even as he'd pulled the trigger, Tom's words had echoed in his head.

But he'd had a choice to make.

There had been no going back.

"You're not going to lose me." Casey smiled at him. The ache in his chest finally eased. "You're going to get the chance to start over with me. No murder. No stories. Just us."

He wanted it to be just them.

The EMT cleared her throat. "Uh, about the hospital…"

Josh pressed his lips to Casey's. "Something you should know…"

She blinked up at him.

"I'm falling for you, too, sweetheart."

Her beautiful smile stretched, lighting her eyes.

"Uh, yeah, I got things here," Tucker called out as he cleared his throat.

Josh's head turned and he found Tucker standing near the open ambulance doors. His friend gave him a little salute. "Why don't you make sure Ms. Quinn gets to the hospital all right? I'm sure she would appreciate an escort. Hayden and I will handle everything at the scene."

He didn't have to be told twice. Josh brought Casey's wrist to his mouth and pressed a kiss to the bruised skin. He felt her pulse surge beneath his lips.

Tucker slammed the ambulance's back doors closed. The siren screamed on. Moments later, they were taking off.

And Josh was holding tight to Casey. The woman he never planned to let go.

Epilogue

Josh Duvane broke from the surface of the water, pulling the regulator out of his mouth and then shoving back his mask. He grabbed for the side of the boat.

"See anything interesting down there?"

He glanced up and straight into the sparking gaze of his new bride. *She married me. She actually married me.*

Casey Quinn—now Casey Quinn-Duvane—smiled at him. He'd never get used to that smile, not in a million years. That smile lit her up from the inside out and it made him feel as if he were staring straight at a miracle.

Maybe because he was. To him, Casey was a miracle. The dream he hadn't even realized he had. The woman who loved him—bright spots and dark.

And he loved her more than anything in the world.

He carefully climbed aboard the boat, then he reached into his bag and pulled out the two perfect sand dollars that he'd just retrieved from the ocean floor. Casey laughed and crowded in closer to him. "Gorgeous!"

He was staring straight at her. "Yes."

She looked up. They were on their honeymoon— sailing in the Florida Keys. The Sandy Shore Killer wasn't in the headlines any longer. Both Finn and Kurt Anderson had survived. Casey had recently covered their stories in an exposé for her new television show.

Kurt was getting counseling. He was putting the pieces of his life back together.

And the town of Hope? It was finally healing. The monsters were gone.

Josh pulled Casey against him. "I love you." He'd never get tired of those words. When he thought of how close he'd come to losing her... Hell, no. He didn't even want to imagine that life. Because *his* life...everything he wanted...she was it.

She rose onto her toes and her lips pressed to his.

* * * * *

Don't miss BEFORE THE DAWN—
the next title in the KILLER INSTINCT *series*
by New York Times *bestselling author*
Cynthia Eden.

Available wherever HQN Books are sold.

Check out the previous books in the
KILLER INSTINCT *series:*

THE GATHERING DUSK
ABDUCTION
AFTER THE DARK

Available now from Harlequin Intrigue
and HQN Books!

Get 2 Free Books,
Plus 2 Free Gifts—
just for trying the Reader Service!

HARLEQUIN
INTRIGUE

"I want to ask you about your babies," Nikki said. "Oakley and
Jesse Rose?" Was it her imagination or did the woman clutch
the dolls even harder to her thin chest?

"What happened the night they disappeared?" Did Nikki
really expect an answer? She could hope, couldn't she? Mostly,
she needed to hear the sound of her voice in this claustrophobic
room. The rocking had a hypnotic effect, like being pulled
down a rabbit hole.

"Everyone outside this room believes you had something to
do with it. You and Nate Corwin." No response, no reaction to
the name. "Was he your lover?"

She moved closer, catching the decaying scent that rose from
the rocking chair as if the woman was already dead. "I don't
believe it's true. But I think you might know who kidnapped
your babies," she whispered.

The speculation at the time was that the kidnapping had been
an inside job. Marianne had been suffering from postpartum
depression. The nanny had said that Mrs. McGraw was having
trouble bonding with the babies and that she'd been afraid to
leave Marianne alone with them.

And, of course, there'd been Marianne's secret lover—the man everyone believed had helped her kidnap her own children. He'd been implicated because of a shovel found in the stables with his bloody fingerprints on it—along with fresh soil—even though no fresh graves had been found.

"Was Nate Corwin involved, Marianne?" The court had decided that Marianne McGraw couldn't have acted alone. To get both babies out the second-story window, she would have needed an accomplice.

"Did my father help you?"

There was no sign that the woman even heard her, let alone recognized her alleged lover's name. And if the woman had answered, Nikki knew she would have jumped out of her skin.

She checked to make sure Tess wasn't watching as she snapped a photo of the woman in the rocker. The flash lit the room for an instant and made a snap sound. As she started to take another, she thought she heard a low growling sound coming from the rocker.

She hurriedly took another photo, though hesitantly, as the growling sound seemed to grow louder. Her eye on the viewfinder, she was still focused on the woman in the rocker when Marianne McGraw seemed to rock forward as if lurching from her chair.

A shriek escaped her before she could pull down the camera. She had closed her eyes and thrown herself back, slamming into the wall. Pain raced up one shoulder. She stifled a scream as she waited for the feel of the woman's clawlike fingers on her throat.

But Marianne McGraw hadn't moved. It had only been a trick of the light. And yet, Nikki noticed something different about the woman.

Marianne was smiling.

Don't miss
DARK HORSE by B.J. Daniels,
available August 2017 wherever
Harlequin® Intrigue books and ebooks are sold.

www.Harlequin.com

Earn points from all your Harlequin book purchases from wherever you shop.

Turn your points into *FREE BOOKS* of your choice
OR
EXCLUSIVE GIFTS from your favorite authors or series.

Join for FREE today at
www.HarlequinMyRewards.com.

Harlequin My Rewards is a free program (no fees) without any commitments or obligations.

MYR17